P50rincess STORIES

Compiled by
TIG THOMAS

Miles
KeLLY

First published in 2017 by Miles Kelly Publishing Ltd
Harding's Barn, Bardfield End Green, Thaxted, Essex, CM6 3PX, UK

2 4 6 8 10 9 7 5 3 1

Publishing Director Belinda Gallagher
Creative Director Jo Cowan
Editorial Director Rosie Neave
Editor Claire Philip
Designer Kayleigh Allen
Editorial Assistant Amy Johnson
Production Elizabeth Collins, Caroline Kelly
Reprographics Stephan Davis, Jennifer Cozens, Thom Allaway
Assets Lorraine King

ISBN 978-1-78617-307-2

Printed in China

British Library Cataloguing-in-Publication Data
A catalogue record for this book is available from the British Library

ACKNOWLEDGEMENTS
The publishers would like to thank the following artists who have contributed to this book:
Kirsten Wilson
The Bright Agency: Smiljana Coh, Cathy Delanssay (cover),
Mélanie Florian, Marcin Piwowarski, Jennie Poh

All other artwork from the Miles Kelly Artwork Bank

The publishers would like to thank the following sources for the use of their photographs:
b/c = back cover, b/g = background, r/t = repeated throughout
Shutterstock.com (b/c) toocrazy; page decorations (r/t) pashabo, asimjp, Alice, lalan;
pp. 12–113: Slobodan Zivkovic, Danussa; pp. 116–217: justaa, vergasova, carla castagno, Yummyphotos;
pp. 220–317: Scott Eric Johnson, Fernando Cortes, Bobb Klissourski; pp. 320–383: Potapov Alexander

Every effort has been made to acknowledge the source and copyright holder of each picture.
Miles Kelly Publishing apologises for any unintentional errors or omissions.

Made with paper from a sustainable forest

www.mileskelly.net

This book belongs to

....

CONTENTS

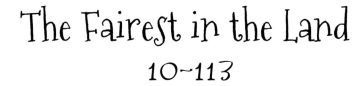

The Fairest in the Land

Enchanting Adventures

Gallant Girls and Brave Lasses

From Rags to Riches

The Fairest in the Land

The Princess Emily

A retelling of **The Knight's Tale**
by Geoffrey Chaucer

ANY YEARS AGO, there lived a noble king called Theseus, with his wife Hippolyta, the queen of the Amazons, and her niece, Princess Emily. Emily was as lovely as a pure white lily upon its stalk of delicate green.

On the first day of May, she awoke early and went to gather flowers and sing about the joys of the morning. She had never looked more lovely, with her hands full of flower blossoms and the sun shining on her beautiful blonde hair.

It just so happened that King Theseus had two knights in his prison. They had been captured fighting against him. Their names were Palamon and Arcite and they were best friends.

On this day, Palamon heard Emily singing and went to look out of the dark window from which he could catch a glimpse of the gardens. He gasped and cried, "A goddess! Surely she must be a goddess! Maybe even Venus, the goddess of love herself." And in that moment Palamon's heart belonged to Emily forever.

Arcite leapt up and looked out of the window for himself.

"That's no goddess!" he cried, "but the most beautiful human the gods have ever made. I shall love her all my life."

"But Arcite," cried Palamon, "I saw her and fell in love with her first. Surely you will respect that?"

"You didn't even know she was a human," said Arcite. "I fell in love with a girl – you only worshipped a goddess."

In just one moment their friendship

was finished forever. Each hoped to win Emily one day, and neither would speak to the other again. Their only joy came from watching Emily walk in the gardens whilst loving her from afar.

Many months later, Arcite's ransom was paid, and King Theseus released him back to his home country of Thebes. There he pined away dreaming only of the beautiful Emily. His face grew pale and his body lost its strength. Then he had an idea.

'No one would know me now,' he thought. 'I shall return to the court of King Theseus as a servant.'

This he did, becoming a squire of King Theseus. His joy was in spending time near Emily, bringing logs in for her fire, watching her dance, sing or talk but never daring to speak to her directly.

After seven long years in prison, Palamon finally escaped. He went to the forest, and one day while he was hiding there, Arcite came riding through on his horse. It was May Day once more, and he had come to gather a woodland garland for Emily's rooms. As he gathered green leaves, he sang a song in praise of his one true love. Suddenly Palamon leapt out of his hiding place and shouted fiercely. "Emily has only one true love and that is I, Palamon!"

The two men then flung themselves upon each other in a desperate rage.

Palamon was like a
raging lion and
Arcite like a hungry
tiger. Heaven
knows how the
fight would have
ended, but King
Theseus came
riding by with the
queen, Princess
Emily and his
court. They found
the two men now apart, panting.

"What's this? Who dares to fight in the
royal forests?" King Theseus cried.

The two men were too angry to be
careful, so they told the king their story.

"So you are Palamon and Arcite," said Theseus at last, "Palamon who has escaped from prison and Arcite who has unlawfully returned to my lands. I condemn you both to immediate death."

With tears in her eyes, Emily slipped off her horse and knelt in front of Theseus. "My Lord," she said, "I beg for the lives of these two young men. It is not their fault that they have been struck by cupid's arrow. I knew nothing of their love, but to kill them would be cruel."

The queen also pleaded with Theseus, and in the end he gave in. "Very well," he said to the two men. "Go back home, collect a hundred knights and return here. We will have a tournament, and the winner shall marry Princess Emily."

So Palamon and Arcite went away to call their friends together, and Emily sat in her high tower room, wondering which man she liked the best.

Theseus built a wonderful arena with stands, a jousting ring and three temples — one to Mars, the god of war, one to Venus, the goddess of love, and one to Diana, the goddess of young maidens. Palamon and Arcite returned the night before the tournament, and each of them went to pray for success.

Arcite went to the temple of war. "Oh great god Mars," he prayed, "Give me victory in tomorrow's fight."

Palamon went to the temple of love.

"Oh gentle goddess," he prayed, "let me win Princess Emily's heart."

Emily went to the temple of Diana. "If I am to marry, let it be to the one who will love me best."

Next day the tournament began. There was a great arranging of armour, fixing of spear-heads, buckling of helmets and polishing of shields. The trumpets sounded the charge. Out flew the swords, gleaming like polished silver. The fight was long, but in the end Palamon was captured and Arcite was declared the winner. Mad with excitement, he threw away his helmet and rode up the field.

But the gods had planned so that all prayers might be answered. Arcite's horse stumbled and fell, throwing him heavily to the ground. He died of his injuries, blessing Emily and begging Palamon's forgiveness with his last breath.

So Palamon won the fair Emily and long did he live in bliss. Emily loved him tenderly, and he served her with so much gentleness that no word of anger was ever heard between them.

Work Hard and Do Well

A traditional story from the Middle East

"He that seeks, shall find, and to him
that knocks, the door shall be opened."

T WAS AN OLD ARABIC PROVERB one
young lad called Abdul had heard
every day of his life, for his mother
was very fond of repeating it. He grew up
trying hard and sure enough, he did
well – as people who try hard usually do.

He worked hard at school, and the

people in his village said he was sure to be successful. Perhaps he might be a wealthy shopkeeper or a trader in pearls, or a successful farmer and own many sheep. But young Abdul was not content with any of this.

One day, as he was tending his father's strip of land, the princess happened to pass through his village in a beautiful carriage. The curtains were closed, but just as the carriage passed Abdul, the camel stumbled, the carriage jolted and the curtain swept aside for a few seconds. It was enough for Abdul to catch a glimpse of the fairest girl in all the land. Her hair was as black and as glossy as a raven's wing, her skin glowed with

the warm colour of honey, and her
expression was of such sweetness
Abdul could think of nothing
else in the world.

He decided to
go to the palace
and ask for the
princess's hand in
marriage. "For,"
he said, "Success
comes to those
who ask for it."
So he
journeyed to
the town and
presented
himself at the

24

palace. The caliph was a good and just man who allowed all his people to visit him. So Abdul was welcomed into the caliph's public room and, bowing before him, made his request.

"O Caliph, I have lived a quiet life and I have never tried to gain anything before. But as my mother repeated to me daily, 'He that seeks, shall find, and to him that knocks, the door shall be opened,' and I have now come to want something with all my heart. I beg you let me marry your daughter!"

The whole court laughed at the idea that a simple village boy might marry their princess and some said he should be punished, but the caliph spoke kindly to the boy and sent him away without punishing him for his boldness. As he went, out of an upper window, the princess watched him go. She sighed and thought she could love such a fine man.

Every day the boy returned, repeating his request and never being put off by the same answer. The caliph began to be tired of Abdul's daily requests and in the end he decided to find a way to stop the boy from coming any more.

He declared, "Why do you deserve to marry my daughter? For me to allow it, you must either be great or wise or brave, or you must have succeeded at some great and difficult task. I will give you a mission so you can prove yourself. Years ago a ruby of great value was lost in the River Tigris. If you find it, you shall have the hand of my daughter."

Abdul was very pleased to hear this. He went to the shores of the Tigris every morning, day after day, to drain the river so he could search the riverbed. Every day he scooped out the water with a bucket and threw it onto the land, working hour after hour until the sun sank down. The fish in the river grew fearful that he might take all their water away, and they went to their king to ask for his help.

"Why is he doing this?" asked the king of the fish.

"He wants the caliph's ruby that lies buried in the bottom of the Tigris."

The Fairest in the Land

"I advise you," said the king of the fish, "to give it to him, for if he is determined to find it, and has a steady will, he will work until he has drained the last drop of water from the Tigris."

The next day, the fish threw the ruby into Abdul's bucket, and he took it to

the caliph. The caliph kept his promise and allowed him to marry the princess. They loved each other dearly, and when the caliph died they ruled the kingdom wisely and well, and worked hard and happily to the end of their days.

The Fair Princess

An extract from
The Enchanted Castle
by E Nesbit

Gerald (also called Jerry), Kathleen and Jimmy find a castle with a maze whilst exploring near their holiday home. At the entrance to the maze they find...

THREAD OF COTTON. Gerald picked it up. One end of it was tied to a thimble with holes in it, and the other end...

"There is no other end," said Gerald. "It's a clue, that's what it is."

He walked forwards, winding the red thread around his fingers as he went. It *was* a clue, and it led them right into the middle of the maze. And in the middle of the maze they came upon The Wonder.

The red clue ran straight across the grass and ended in a small hand with jewelled rings on every finger. The hand was, naturally, attached to an arm. The arm wore a sleeve of pink and gold silk, and the sleeve was part of a dress. The dress was worn by a girl who lay asleep on a stone seat. A thin veil spangled with silver stars covered her face.

"It's Sleeping Beauty," said Kathleen.

"Look how old-fashioned her clothes are. She has slept for a hundred years. Gerald, you're the eldest, you must be the prince."

"She isn't really a princess," said Jimmy. But the others laughed at him, partly because him saying things like that was enough to spoil any game, and partly because they weren't sure if she might actually be a princess.

"Lift the veil up, Jerry," said Kathleen in a whisper.

"Lift it yourself," said Gerald.

She very gently lifted the edge of the veil and turned it back. The princess's face was small and white between long plaits of black hair. Her nose was straight and her eyebrows were finely traced.

"Now then," urged Kathleen. "Jerry, don't be silly. You've got to do it."

"Do what?" asked Gerald, kicking his left boot with his right.

"Why, kiss her awake, of course." said Kathleen.

"Not me!" was Gerald's quick reply.

"I'd do it," said Kathleen, "but I don't suppose it'd make any difference."

She did it – and it didn't. The princess still lay in a deep slumber.

"Then you must, Jimmy. Jump back quickly before she can hit you."

"She won't hit him, he's such a little chap," said Gerald.

"Little yourself!" said Jimmy. "I don't mind kissing her. I'm not a coward, like Some People. Only if I do, I'm going to be the leader for the rest of the day."

"Now look here, hold on!" cried Gerald, "perhaps I'd better..."

But, in the meantime, Jimmy had planted a loud, cheerful-sounding kiss on the princess's pale cheek, and now the three stood breathless, awaiting the result.

And the result was that the princess opened her large, dark eyes, stretched out her arms, yawned a little, covered her mouth with a small hand, and said, quite distinctly, "Then the hundred years are over? How the yew hedges have grown! Which of you is my prince? Who woke me from my long, deep slumber?

"I did," said Jimmy fearlessly.

"My noble preserver!" said the princess.

"But I say," said he, "you aren't really a princess, are you?"

"Of course I am," she answered, "who else could I be? Look at my crown!"

"But..." said Jimmy.

"I say," Gerald said, "do you really believe in magic, and all that?"

"I ought to," she said, "if anybody does. Look, here is the place where I pricked my finger with the spindle."

"Is this really is an enchanted castle?"

"Of course it is," said the princess. "How stupid you are!" She stood up, and her pink brocaded dress lay in bright waves about her feet.

"I don't believe you're a princess at all," said Jimmy.

"Don't believe it then, if you don't want to," said the princess, and she turned to the others.

"Let's go back to the castle," she said, "and I'll show you all my lovely jewels and things."

"Yes," said Gerald hesitantly. "But..."

"But what?" The princess's tone was becoming impatient.

"But we're most awfully hungry."

"Oh, so am I!" cried the princess.

"We've had nothing to eat since breakfast this morning."

"And it's three now," said the princess, looking at the sundial. "Why, you've had nothing to eat for hours. But think of me! I haven't had anything to eat for a hundred years. Come along to the castle."

"The mice will have eaten everything," said Jimmy, sadly.

"Not they," cried the princess joyously. "Everything's enchanted here. Time stood still for a hundred years. Come along. One of you must carry my train."

The Fair Princess

They walked in a slow procession along the grass towards the castle. The princess went first, and Kathleen carried her shining train, then came Jimmy, and Gerald came last. They were all quite sure that they had walked right into the middle of a fairytale. They found themselves in a big hall, with suits of armour around the walls. The princess turned to the three children and said, "Just wait here a minute, and mind you don't talk while I'm away. This castle is full of magic, and I don't know what will happen if you talk."

Jimmy wanted very much to say that he didn't believe anything would happen at all, only he was afraid something would happen if he did, so he merely made a face and stuck out his tongue.

Then the princess came slowly back, kicking her long skirts in front of her. She was carrying a large tray, which she set down on the end of a long table, and breathed a huge sigh of relief.

"Oh! It was heavy," she said. The tray held a loaf of bread, a lump of cheese and a jug of water. A pile of plates, mugs and knives added to its weight.

"Come along," said the princess hospitably. "I couldn't find anything but bread and cheese, but it doesn't matter because everything's magic here, and unless you have some dreadful secret fault the bread and cheese will turn into anything you like. What would you like?" she asked Kathleen.

"Roast chicken," said Kathleen, without a slight hesitation.

The princess cut a slice of bread and laid it on a dish.

"There you are," she said, "roast chicken. Shall I carve it, or will you?"

"You, please," said Kathleen, and she

received a piece of dry bread on a plate.

"Green peas?" asked the princess, and she laid another piece beside the bread.

Kathleen began to eat the bread, cutting it up with a knife and fork as you would eat chicken. It was no use owning up that she didn't see any chicken and peas because that would be admitting that she had some dreadful secret fault.

'If I have, it is a secret, even from me,' she told herself.

The others asked for roast beef and cabbage and got it, she supposed, though to her it only looked like bread and cheese.

'I wonder what my secret fault is,' she thought, as the princess remarked that she would like a slice of roast peacock.

"It's a game, isn't it?" asked Jimmy.

"What's a game?" asked the princess.

"Pretending it's beef, the bread and cheese, I mean."

"A game? But it is beef. Look at it," said the princess, opening her eyes wide.

"Yes, of course," said Jimmy feebly. "I was only joking."

Bread and cheese is not perhaps so good as roast beef or chicken or peacock, but very much better than nothing. They all ate and drank and felt much better.

The Minstrel's Song

By Maud Lindsay

NCE, LONG, LONG AGO, in a country over the sea there lived a prince called René, who married a lovely princess called Imogen.

Imogen came across the sea to the prince's beautiful country, and all his people welcomed her with great joy because the prince loved her.

"What can I do to please you today?" the prince asked her every morning. One day the princess answered that she would like to hear all the minstrels in the prince's country, for they were said to be the finest in the world.

As soon as the prince heard this, he called his heralds and sent them throughout his land to sound their trumpets and call aloud, "Hear you minstrels! Prince René bids you come to play at his court on May Day, for love of the princess."

The minstrels were men who sang beautiful songs and played harps, and long ago they went about from place to place, from castle to castle, from palace to palace, and were always sure of a welcome wherever they roamed.

They could sing of the brave deeds of knights, and of wars and battles, and could tell of the mighty hunters who hunted in the great forests, and of fairies and goblins, better than a storybook. And because there were no storybooks in those days, everybody was glad to see them come.

So when the minstrels heard the prince's message, they hurried to the palace on May Day, and it so happened that some of them met on the way and decided to travel along together.

The Minstrel's Song

One of these minstrels was a young man named Harmonius. While the others talked of the songs they would sing, he gathered wildflowers from the roadside.

"I can sing of the drums and battles," said the oldest minstrel, whose hair was white and whose step was slow.

"I can sing of ladies and their fair faces," said the youngest minstrel, but Harmonius whispered, "Stop and listen! Listen!"

"We hear nothing at all but the wind in the tree-tops," said the others. "We have no time to stop."

They hurried on and left Harmonius. He stood under the trees and listened, for he heard something very sweet. At last he realized that it was the wind singing of its travels through the world, telling how it raced over the sea, tossing the waves and rocking the ships, and hurried on to the hills, where the trees made harps of their branches, and then how it blew down into the valleys, where all the flowers danced in time.

Harmonius listened until he knew the whole song, and then he ran on to reach his friends, who were still talking of the grand sights that they were to about to see.

"We shall see the prince and speak to him," said the oldest minstrel.

"And his golden crown and the princess's jewels," added the youngest.

48

Harmonius had no chance to tell of the wind's song.

Now their path led them through the wood. As they talked, Harmonius said, "Hush! Listen!" But the others said, "Oh! That is only the sound of the brook trickling over the stones. Let us make haste to the prince's court."

But Harmonius stayed to hear the joyful song that the brook was singing, of its journey through mosses and ferns and shady ways, and

of tumbling over the rocks in shining
waterfalls on its long journey to the sea.

Harmonius sat and listened until he
knew every word of the song of by heart,
and then he hurried on to catch up with
the others.

When he reached the others once more,
they were still talking of the prince and
princess, so he could not tell them of the
brook. Then he heard something once
again that was wonderfully sweet, and he
cried, "Listen! Listen!"

"Oh! That is only a bird!" the others
replied. "Let us make haste to the court, it
is not far now."

But Harmonius would not go, for the
bird sang so joyfully that Harmonius

laughed aloud when
he heard its song.

The bird was singing
a song of green
trees, and in
every tree a nest, and
in every nest some eggs!

"Thank you, little bird," he said, "you
have taught me a song." And he made
haste to join his friends, for by this time
they were very near the palace.

When they arrived, they received a
hearty welcome and feasted in the great
hall before they came before the prince.

The prince and princess sat on their
thrones. The prince thought of the
princess and the minstrels, but the

princess thought of her old home, and of the butterflies she had chased when she was a little child. One by one the minstrels played their harps before them.

The oldest minstrel sang of battles and drums, just as he had said he would. The youngest minstrel sang of ladies and their fair faces, which pleased the court ladies very much.

Then came Harmonius. When he touched his harp and sang, the song sounded like the wind blowing, the sea roaring and the trees creaking. Then it grew very soft, and sounded like a trickling brook dripping on stones and running over little pebbles, and while the prince and princess and all the court listened in surprise, Harmonius's song grew sweeter, sweeter, sweeter. It was as if you heard all the birds in spring. And then the song was over.

The princess clapped her hands, and the ladies waved their handkerchiefs. The prince came down from his throne to ask Harmonius if he came from fairyland with such a wonderful song. But Harmonius answered, "Three singers sang along the way, and I learnt the song from them today."

Now, all the other minstrels looked up in surprise when Harmonius spoke, and the oldest minstrel said to the prince, "Harmonius is dreaming! We heard no music on our way today."

And the youngest minstrel said, "Harmonius is surely mad! We met nobody on our way today."

But the princess said, "That is an old, old song. I heard it when I was a little child, and I can name the three singers." And so she did. Can you name them too?

Answer: The wind, the brook and the bird

How Princess Angelica Took a Little Maid

An extract from **The Rose and the Ring**
by William Makepeace Thackeray

This is an extract from a longer
story about two very different girls.

ONE DAY, when Princess Angelica was still quite a little girl, she was walking in the garden of the palace with Mrs Gruffanuff, the

governess. Angelica was carrying a bun to feed the swans and ducks in the royal pond.

Angelica had not yet reached the duck pond, when a funny little girl came toddling up. She had a great quantity of hair blowing about her chubby little cheeks, and she looked as if she had not been washed for a long while. The little girl wore a ragged bit of a cloak, and only one shoe.

"You little wretch, who on earth let you in here?" asked Mrs Gruffanuff angrily.

"Div me dat bun," said the little girl, "me vely hungy."

"Hungry! What is that?" asked Princess Angelica, and gave the child the bun.

"Oh, Princess!" said Mrs Gruffanuff, "How good, how truly angelical you are! See, Your Majesties," she said to the king and queen, who now came walking up to them, "how kind the princess is! She met this little wretch in the garden — I can't tell you why the guards did not stop her at the gate — and the dear princess has given her the whole of her bun!"

"But Mrs Gruffanuff, I didn't want it," said Angelica.

"You are a darling little angel all the same," said the governess.

"Yes, I know I am," said Angelica. "Dirty little girl, don't you think I am very pretty?" Indeed, she had on the finest of little dresses, and, as her hair was carefully curled, she looked very well.

"Oh, pooty, pooty!" said the little girl, laughing, dancing and munching her bun. As she ate it she began to sing, "Oh, what fun to have a plum bun! How I wis it never was done!" At which they all began to laugh merrily.

"I can dance as well as sing," said the little girl. "I can dance, and I can sing, and I can do all sorts of ting." And she ran to a flowerbed, pulled out some flowers, made herself a little wreath, and danced before the king and queen so comically and prettily, that everybody was delighted.

"Who was your mother – who were your relations, little girl?" said the queen.

The little girl said, "Little lion was my brudder, great big lioness my mudder, neber heard of any udder."

So Angelica said to the queen, "My parrot flew away out of its cage yesterday, and I no longer care for any of my toys. I think this little dirty child will amuse me. I will take her home, and give her my old frocks…"

"Oh, the generous darling!" said Mrs Gruffanuff.

"...which I have worn ever so many times, and am quite tired of," Angelica went on, "and she shall be my maid. Will you come home with me, little girl?"

The child clapped her hands, and said, "Go home with you — yes!"

And they all laughed again, and took the child to the palace. The little girl was given a bath, and once

washed and combed she looked as pretty as Angelica, almost. Not that Angelica ever thought so, for this little lady never imagined that anybody in the world could be as pretty, as good or as clever as her fine self.

In order that the little girl should not become too proud, Mrs Gruffanuff took her old ragged cloak and one shoe, and put them into a glass box. A card laid upon them, upon which was written,

These were the old clothes in which little Betsinda was found when the great goodness and admirable kindness of Her Royal Highness the Princess Angelica received this little outcast.

And the date was added, and the box locked up.

For a while little Betsinda was a great favourite with the princess. She danced, sang, and made little rhymes to amuse her mistress. But then the princess got a monkey, and afterwards a little dog. After that she got a doll, and did not care for Betsinda any more. Betsinda became very quiet and sang no more funny songs, because nobody cared to hear her.

And then, as she grew older, she was made a little lady's maid to the princess, and though she had no wages, she worked and mended, and put Angelica's hair in papers, and was never cross when scolded, and was always eager to please.

She was always up early and to bed late, and at hand when wanted, and in fact became a perfect little maid.

So the two girls grew up, and Betsinda was never tired of waiting on the princess. She made her dresses better than the best dress-maker, and was useful in many ways.

Whilst the princess was having her lessons, Betsinda would watch, and in 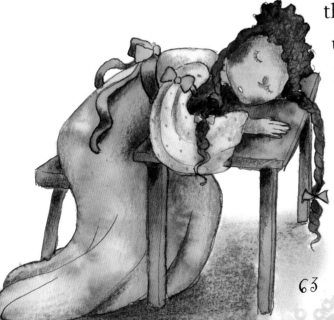 this way she picked up a great deal of learning – for she was always awake, though her mistress was not, and listened to the wise professors when Angelica was snoozing or thinking of the next ball.

And when the dancing-master came, Betsinda learned along with Angelica, and when the music-master came, she watched him and practised the princess's pieces when Angelica was away at balls and parties. When the drawing-master came she took note of all he said and did — and the same with French, Italian and all the other languages.

When the princess was going out in the evening she would say, "Betsinda, you may as well finish what I have begun."

"Yes, miss," Betsinda would say, and sit down very cheerfully, not to FINISH what Angelica began, but to DO it.

For instance, the princess would begin to draw, let us say, a head of a warrior, but Betsinda would finish it. The princess would put her name to the drawing, and the court and king and queen would admire it, saying, "Was there ever a genius like Angelica?"

So, I am sorry to say, was it with the princess's embroidery and other accomplishments. Angelica actually believed that she did these things herself, and received all the flattery of the court as if every word of it was true. Thus she began to think that there was no young woman in all the world equal to herself, and that no young man was good enough for her. As for Betsinda, she heard none of these praises, so she was not puffed up by them, and being a most grateful, good-natured girl, she was only too anxious to do everything that might give her mistress pleasure. Now you begin to perceive that Angelica had faults of her own, and was by no means such a wonder of wonders as many people represented Her Royal Highness to be.

Princess Hyacinth

A traditional Russian fairy tale

ONCE UPON A TIME there was a good and brave prince called Milan who rode out with his horse seeking adventures. On the third day he came to a lake. Thirty ducks were swimming on its smooth surface, while spread about upon the grass were thirty white dresses. The prince dismounted, and taking up one of the garments, seated himself behind a bush and waited to see what would happen. The ducks dived under the water and swam around for a time, then came ashore and putting on the little white garments, became beautiful maidens, and disappeared. But there was one little duck that remained on the lake and swam about uttering miserable cries.

The prince came out from behind the bush holding the dress and the little duck begged him to give it back to her. As soon as he passed it to her, the loveliest maiden he had ever seen stood before him. They talked and walked together and at the end of an hour the prince was deeply in love. He begged to see her father so he could ask for her hand in marriage.

"I wish it may go well," said she. "My name is Hyacinth, and I am one of the thirty daughters of a King of the Underworld, to whose castle I will lead you. Approach him on your knees and do not fear him, for I will be there to help you, whatever happens."

She tapped her little foot on the ground, which opened, and they were transported to the palace of her father. When his eyes became used to the light, the prince saw the monstrous king sitting on a dazzling throne. His green eyes looked out from under a golden crown, and his hideous claws clutched the air with rage when he saw the prince. Remembering what the maiden had told him, Prince Milan

walked boldly up to the throne and knelt
at the feet of the king, and told his story.

"If you want to marry my daughter,"
the king replied, "then tonight you must
build me a palace of
gold and marble, with
windows of crystal, and
all about it the most
beautiful gardens — or
I shall cut off your head."

The prince went back to
his chamber to await his
doom, for the task was
impossible. But later a bee
flew into his chamber, and
as it entered the room it
became Hyacinth.

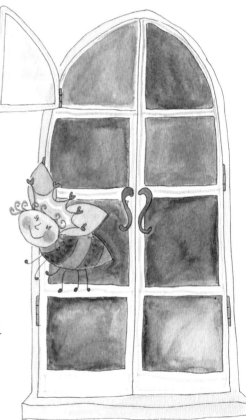

"Why are you sad, Prince Milan?" she asked. He told her of her father's impossible command and added, "Naturally, I am not happy at the thought of losing my head."

"Do not be distressed," said she, "but trust in me, for I have studied magic."

In the morning he looked out of the window and saw a wonderful marble palace with a gold roof. It had windows of crystal, and all about it were the most beautiful gardens he had ever seen.

The king was greatly astonished, but not yet satisfied — he required of the prince another task still.

"If, before this candle burns to the bottom," said he, "you can make me a

pair of boots reaching to my knees,
I will let you go — but if you cannot, you
will lose your head."

"Then we must fly, for I love you
dearly," said Hyacinth, when the prince
had told her of this new task. She
breathed on the windowpane, and
straightaway it was covered with icy
frost. Then, leading Prince Milan from
the chamber, she locked the door, and
they fled through the same passage by
which they had entered the Underworld.
Beside the smooth lake his horse was still
grazing, and mounting it, they were
borne swiftly away.

When the king sent for the prince,
Hyacinth's frozen breath on the

windowpane answered the messengers through the door, and so delayed the discovery of their escape. At last the magician lost patience, ordered the door burst open and sent men after them.

"I hear horses' feet behind us," said Hyacinth. She changed herself into a river, the prince became a bridge, and his horse a blackbird. Their pursuers, no longer finding their footprints, returned to the king, who cursed them, and sent them out again.

"I hear horses' feet behind us," said Hyacinth for the second time. She changed herself, the prince and the horse into a dense forest with many paths, so that the followers were bewildered, and they again returned to the king. But the king sent them out again.

"I hear horses' feet behind us," said Hyacinth for the third time. This time it was the king himself. Hyacinth took the little cross from the neck of the prince, and changed herself into a church, the prince into a monk and the horse into the belfry, so that the king lost all trace of them, and returned to the Underworld.

When he had departed, the prince and Hyacinth mounted the horse and rode till they came to a beautiful town.

"We must not enter," said she, "for we may not come out again." But the prince would not take her advice, and insisted upon passing through the gates.

"Then," the maiden replied, "when the royal family come out to meet you, do not kiss the hand of the princess or you will become enchanted, forget me and never come back. I will become a milestone and wait for you here."

It was all as Hyacinth had said. The king and queen, with their daughter and son, came out to greet him, and when the princess held out her hand, Prince Milan kissed it and forgot Hyacinth.

The first and second day went by, and when the third day came, Hyacinth wept, and became a little blue flower growing by the roadside. An old man came along, dug up the flower and carried it home. He planted it in his garden, watered it and tended it carefully. One day the little flower became a beautiful maiden.

"Thank you for not leaving me to die by the roadside," she said, and she told the old man her story.

"Tomorrow is Prince Milan's wedding day," said the old man, "You must hurry."

Hyacinth at once went to the palace cook and asked if she could make the prince a cake. The cook was so struck with her beauty that he could not refuse the request.

That evening, Prince Milan was called upon to cut the cake for his guests. As soon as he had done so, out flew two white doves.

"Dear love," cried one, "do not leave me as Prince Milan left Hyacinth."

The prince suddenly remembered all
that he had forgotten and ran from the
room. At the door he found Hyacinth and
his horse awaiting him. They mounted
and rode swiftly away to his kingdom,
where the king and queen received them
with tears of joy, and they lived in
happiness to the end of their days.

The Princess and her Grandmother

An extract from **The Princess and the Goblin**
by George MacDonald

Princess Irene lives in a remote castle-house. One night,
while exploring the empty rooms, she goes looking for
someone magical that she has met once before.

ONE MORNING the nurse left Irene
with the housekeeper for a while.
To amuse her she turned out the
contents of an old cabinet upon the table.

The little princess sat playing with them for two hours or more. But while handling an old-fashioned brooch she ran the pin of it into her thumb, and gave a little scream with the sharpness of the pain. She would have thought little more of it had the pain not increased and her thumb begun to swell. The nurse was fetched, the doctor was sent for, and she was put to bed. The pain still continued, and although she fell asleep and dreamed many dreams, the pain was always there. At last it woke her up.

The moon was shining brightly into the room. Irene's hand was burning hot and she fancied if she could hold it into the moonlight that would cool it. She went

through the nursery to go to the
window. But when she came to
the foot of the old staircase there
was the moon shining down,
and making the worm-eaten oak
look very strange and delicate
and lovely. In a moment she was
putting her little feet one after the
other in the silvery path up the
staircase. Some little girls

would have been afraid to be alone in the middle of the night, but not Irene, for she was a princess.

So up and up she went, stair after stair, until she came to the many rooms — all just as she had seen them before. Through passage after passage she softly sped. As if she had known every step of the way, she walked straight to the door at the foot of the narrow stair that led to the tower.

"What if I should find my beautiful old grandmother up there!" she said to herself as she crept up the steps.

When she reached the top she stood a moment listening in the dark. Yes! It was the hum of the spinning wheel! She tapped gently at the door.

"Come in, Irene," said the sweet voice.

The princess opened the door and entered. In the middle of the moonlight sat the old lady in her black dress with the white lace, and her silvery hair mingling with the moonlight, so that you could not have told which was which. "Come in, Irene," she said again. "Can you tell me what I am spinning?"

"No," Irene said, "I don't know what you are spinning. I thought that you were a dream. Why couldn't I find you before, great-great-grandmother?"

"You would have found me sooner if you hadn't come to think I was a dream."

All the time they talked the old lady kept on spinning.

"You haven't told me yet what I am spinning," she said.

"I don't know. It's very pretty stuff."

It was indeed very pretty stuff. There was a good bunch of it on the distaff — the rod on which wool is held — attached to the spinning wheel, and in the moonlight it shone grey rather than white, and glittered only a little.

"I am spinning this for you, my child."

"For me! What am I to do with it?"

"I will tell you. But first I will tell you what it is. It is spiderweb — of a particular kind. There is only one forest where the spiders live who make this particular kind — the finest and strongest of any."

"Do you work all day and night, too, great-great-great-great-grandmother?" said the princess, thinking to be very polite with so many greats.

"I am not quite so great as all that," the old lady said, smiling. "If you call me grandmother, that will do. No, only moonlit nights. I shan't work much longer tonight."

"What will you do next, grandmother?"

"Go to bed I should think. Would you like to see my bedroom?"

"Yes, I would."

"Then I think I won't work any longer tonight. We can go there now."

The old lady rose, and took Irene by the hand, but it was her bad hand and Irene gave a little cry of pain. "My child!" said her grandmother, "what is the matter?"

Irene held her hand into the moonlight, and told her all about it. Her grandmother said, "Give me your other hand," and, having led her out upon the landing, opened the door on the opposite side.

What was Irene's surprise to see the loveliest room she had ever seen in her

life! It was large and lofty, and
dome-shaped. From the centre hung a
lamp as round as a ball, shining as if
with the brightest moonlight. A large
oval bed stood in the middle, with a
rose-coloured blanket, and lovely pale
blue velvet curtains.

The walls were also blue — spangled all
over with stars of silver.

The old lady left her and, going to a
strange-looking cabinet, opened it and
took out a silver casket. Then she sat
down on a low chair and, calling Irene,
she looked at her hand. Having examined
it, she opened the casket, and took from it
a little ointment. The sweetest scent filled
the room — like that of roses and lilies —

as she rubbed the ointment gently all over the hot, swollen hand. Her touch was so pleasant and cool that it seemed to drive away the pain and heat.

"Oh, grandmother! It is so nice!" said Irene. "Thank you, thank you."

Then the old lady took out a large handkerchief, which she carefully tied around Irene's hand.

"Would you like to stay here with me?"

"Oh, yes, dear grandmother," said Irene.

So she got a large silver basin, and made Irene sit on the chair, and washed her feet. This done, she was ready for bed. And oh, what a delicious bed it was into which her grandmother laid her! She hardly could have told she was lying

upon anything — she felt nothing but
wonderful softness.

The old lady lay down beside her and
the little princess nestled close to her
grandmother, who took her in both her
arms and held her close.

"Oh, dear! This is so nice!" said the princess. "I didn't know anything in the world could be so comfortable. I should like to lie here forever."

Just a moment later the little princess was dreaming in the midst of the loveliest dreams. But no dream could be more lovely than what she had left behind when she fell asleep. In the morning she found herself back in her own bed. There was no handkerchief or anything else on her hand, only a sweet scent lingered. The swelling had all gone down — in fact, her hand was perfectly well.

The Flower Princess

Anon

HERE WAS ONCE a princess so fair and lovely that the sun shone more brightly on her than on anyone else, the river stopped running when she walked by so that it might gaze on her beauty, and birds sang underneath her window at night.

Princes came to beg for her hand in marriage, but she swore she would only marry a prince who was kind, good and true. Many princes tried to convince her of their fine qualities, but none succeeded — until one day a prince from a small kingdom came to woo her. He fell in love with her, she could not resist him, and they were married. She wore a silver dress embroidered with crystal drops and looked lovely. The court scattered her path with rose petals and threw sugar sweets as the couple walked past.

But alas, trouble can come to all of us. The prince's kingdom had an evil fairy. She was very beautiful but her beauty was spoilt by the cruelty and mean thoughts that she held inside.

When she saw the princess with her sweet and good face, her heart filled with jealousy and rage. She wove a spell to transform the princess into a flower in a nearby meadow.

The spell was not powerful enough to conquer the princess completely, so by night she appeared again in her true form, but every morning she had to transform into her flowery shape and spend the day standing among the grasses and the other flowers.

The Fairest in the Land

One night she overheard the fairy talking and learnt how to break the spell. She told her husband, "If you come to the meadow in the morning and pick me the spell will be broken forever."

"How will I know which one is you?" he said. The princess did not know, for her shape changed every day.

That morning she changed into a flower and the prince hastened to the field to try and find his love. He walked among the grasses and the many flowers. How could he find his love?

Then a thought came to him and he looked closely at each bloom. Finally he stopped before a blue cornflower, touched it gently with his fingers, plucked it and carried it back to his palace. As he passed through the gates, the flower fell to the ground and his princess stood before him.

"How did you find me?" she asked.

"Dew had fallen on all of the other flowers," he replied, "you alone had no dew upon you, for you had spent the night at the palace."

The Princess and the Raven

An extract from **The Wonder Clock**
by Howard Pyle

ONCE UPON A TIME there was a king who had three daughters — the two eldest were handsome, but the youngest, whose name was Golden Hair, was the prettiest maiden to be found within the four ends of the earth.

One day the king went out hunting with all his people. Towards evening he

found himself
alone and lost
in the forest.
The further he
went, the less able
he was to find the road home again. As
the king wandered he came to a tree
where a great raven sat. It was as
black as chimney soot
and had eyes that
glowed like two
burning coals.

"And where are you going,
King?" said the black raven.

"I don't know," said the king, "For I am lost and don't know the way home."

"See now," said the raven, "I will show you the way, if you will give me your youngest daughter to be my wife."

"Oh, no," said the king, "I can never do such a thing as that."

"Very well, then," said the raven, "off I go, and here you will have to stay."

Now one will do much before one will stay in a dark forest forever, and so the king promised at last that if the raven would show him the way home, it should have Princess Golden Hair for its wife. So the raven showed him the way out.

"Tomorrow," it said, "I'll come for my bride, your youngest daughter."

When the next morning came, there was the great black raven sitting outside of the castle gateway waiting for Princess Golden Hair to be sent to him.

But it was not the princess whom he got after all, for the king had told the shepherd to dress his daughter in the princess's dress, and it was she who went to the great black raven. The raven took the shepherd's daughter on its back and away it flew over woods and meadows, until it came to a little hut that stood on a bleak hill. In the hut was a table, and on the table stood a golden goblet of red wine, a silver cup of white wine, and an earthenware jug full of bitter beer.

"This is our home," said the raven, "and

now will my dear one drink refreshment after her long and tiresome journey?"

The shepherd's daughter went to the table and took a good drink of the beer. The raven knew that she was no true princess to be happy with bitter beer out of an earthenware jug, when she could have good red wine from a golden goblet. "Come," said the raven, "home we go!" He took her upon his back and flew until they arrived back at the king's castle.

"See," said the raven, "this is not the one I want. Let me have my true bride or you will suffer for it."

The king was frightened. "Very well," said he, "come tomorrow and you shall have your true bride."

When the next morning came, there was the raven waiting. But it was not the princess that he got. The king had ordered the steward's daughter to wear one of the princess's dresses. So the raven took her on his back and flew till he came to the little hut on top of the bleak hill. There stood the golden goblet, the silver cup and the earthenware jug just as before. And now would not the dear maiden drink a drop after her long journey?

Yes, indeed, so she took a good drink of the white wine in the silver cup. But the raven saw that she was no true princess, or she would never have been contented with the silver cup. "Come," said he, "home we go again, for you are not the bride I seek." So away he flew to the king's castle. "Tomorrow morning," he said to the king, "I will come for the true princess again, and if I do not get her this time you will suffer, for I will tear down your castle about your ears!"

Now the king was terribly frightened. The next morning when the raven came it was Princess Golden Hair herself whom he got. Up he took her on his back and away he flew with her. The princess did nothing but weep, so when they came to the little hut, she was glad enough to drink a drop. She didn't look at the earthenware jug or the silver cup, but going straight to the golden goblet she drank the good red wine.

The Fairest in the Land

Then all of a sudden the hut grew until it changed into a splendid castle. The black raven changed into the most handsome prince in the world. He kissed Princess Golden Hair and said, "I have found my true bride. You have freed me and my castle and all of my people from an enchantment. My wicked stepmother laid spells upon us that could only be broken when a real princess drank from the golden goblet."

Then they were married, and a fine wedding they had of it, I can tell you.

How the Princess was Beaten in a Race

By Horace E Scudder

HERE WAS ONCE A KING who had a daughter, and this daughter was very fair. Every prince in all the countries around wished to marry her. Now the princess was a very swift runner and she ran so fast that no one could overtake her.

How the Princess was Beaten in a Race

The king was in no hurry for his daughter to marry, so he announced to the kingdom that no one should have her for a wife who could not beat her in a running race. Anyone, prince or peasant, might try their luck. The first man who beat her in the race should marry her, but whoever raced and did not win must have his head cut off!

At first there were many who tried, for a great many princes were in love with the princess. Even men who were not princes thought they might outrun her, and become as good as princes.

The girl had fine fun. She raced with each one and she always beat everyone in the game. A great many heads were cut off, and at last it was hard to find anyone who dared to race with her. But there was one poor young man in the country who thought to himself, 'I am poor, and have only my head to lose if I do not win the race. But if I should win, I should become noble, and all my family would be noble also.'

He was a good runner, and a fellow of quick wit. He heard that the princess was very fond of roses, so he gathered a fine bunch. He also had a silken belt made. Finally he took all his money and bought a silken bag, and placed in it a golden ball. On the ball were the words 'Who plays with me shall never tire of play.'

These three things he placed in a pocket

of his robe. He then went and knocked at the palace gate. The porter asked him what he wished, and he said he had come to race the princess.

The princess herself, who was only a young girl, looked out over the edge of the balcony and heard what was said. She saw that he was poorly dressed, so she looked on him with scorn.

But the king's law made no choice between rich and poor, prince and peasant. So the princess got ready to run. The king and all the court gathered to see the race, and the headsman went off to sharpen his axe.

The two had not run far, and the princess was outrunning the young man, when he drew forth his bunch of roses. He threw it so that it fell at the feet of the princess. She stopped, picked it up, and was greatly pleased with the flowers. She looked at them, smelled them, and began to bind them in her hair. The princess forgot all about the race, when suddenly she saw the young man far ahead of her.

At once she tore the roses off, threw them from her, and ran like the wind. It was but a little while before she overtook the young man. She tapped him lightly on the shoulder and said, "Stop, foolish boy! How dare you hope to marry me!"

But as she sped past him, he threw before her the silken belt. Again she stopped, and stooped to look at it. It was a beautiful belt, and she clasped it about her waist. As she was buckling it, she saw the young man nearing the finish line.

"Wretch!" she cried, and burst into tears. Then she flung the girdle away and bounded forwards. Once more she caught up with him. She seized him by the arm.

"You shall not marry me!" she said angrily, and sprang past him. The princess was near the finish line, but the young man now let the silken bag fall at her feet. The ball of gold glittered in it, and the princess was curious to see what the plaything was. She paused for just a moment, raised the bag from the ground and took out the ball. It had words on it, and she stood still to read them, "'Who plays with me shall never tire of play'. I should like to see if that is true," said the princess, and she began to play with the ball. She tossed it in the air over and over, and no one can say if she would have tired, for suddenly she

112

heard a great shout. The young man had reached the winning post first and his head was safe. He married the princess and all his family were made noble, as he had wished.

Enchanting Adventures

The Three Dogs

By the Brothers Grimm

THERE WAS ONCE A SHEPHERD who had a son and a daughter. On his deathbed he said, "I have nothing to leave you but three sheep and a house — divide them between you, as you like."

The brother asked his sister which she would like best, and she chose the house.

"Then I'll take the sheep and go out to seek my fortune," he said.

One day on his travels, he met a man

with three dogs, at a crossroad.

"Hello, my fine fellow," said the man, "I see you have three sheep. If you'll give them to me, I'll give you my three dogs."

The youth smiled and replied, "What would I do with your dogs?"

"My dogs are not like other dogs," said the stranger. "The smallest one is called Salt, and will bring you food whenever you wish, the second is called Pepper, and will tear anyone who tries to hurt you to pieces. The biggest one is called Mustard, and he is so powerful that he can break iron with his teeth."

The shepherd happily gave the stranger his sheep. Every day Salt brought him a fine meal and he went along merrily.

One day he met
a carriage, all draped in black.
Inside sat a beautiful girl, crying. The
coachman told him that a dragon lived
nearby, and every year it ate a
maiden. This year its choice had
fallen on the king's daughter.

The shepherd felt sad and decided to
follow the carriage. After a while it
stopped and the girl got out. When she
had walked halfway up
the hill, a terrible-
looking monster

with the body of a snake, and with huge wings and claws, came towards her. The shepherd called, "Pepper, come to the rescue," and the second dog set upon the dragon, and after a fierce struggle bit it so sharply in the neck that the monster breathed its last breath. Then the dog ate up the dragon's body, except for its two front teeth, which the shepherd picked up and put in his pocket.

The princess begged the shepherd to return with her to her father, who would reward him richly. But the youth said that he wanted to see something of the world, and that he would return again in three years' time. So, bidding each other farewell, she and the shepherd separated.

But while the princess was driving home the carriage suddenly stood still, and the coachman turned to her and said, "You must tell your father that it was I who killed the dragon, or I will throw

you into the river, and no one will be any
the wiser, for they will think the dragon
has devoured you."

The princess was in a dreadful state
when she heard these words, but there
was nothing she could do but to promise.
They returned to the capital, and
everyone was delighted when they saw
the princess. The king hugged his
daughter with tears of joy, and turning to
the coachman said, "You have saved the
life of my precious child, you shall be
rewarded. Take her for your wife, but as
she is still so young, do not let the
wedding happen for another year."

The poor princess wept bitterly, but she
could not break her promise. When the

year was over, she begged hard for
another. When this year passed also, she
begged so hard for one more year that the
king's heart melted, and he agreed, much
to the princess's joy, for she knew that her
real rescuer would appear at the end of
the third year. And so the year passed
away, and the wedding day was fixed,
and all the people were prepared to make
merry and feast.

   On the wedding day the shepherd
returned with his three black dogs. He
asked what was the meaning of all the
feasting and celebration, and they told
him that the king's daughter was going to
be married to the man who had killed the
dragon. The shepherd at once announced

that the coachman was a liar, but no one would listen to him, and he was thrown into a cell with iron doors for causing trouble on the wedding day.

While he was lying there, planning how to escape, an idea dawned on him, and he called out, "Mustard, come to my help," and before he could count to two the creature had bitten through the iron bars and stood beside him.

The king had just arrived at the church, when the shepherd appeared. The former coachman grew as white as a sheet when he saw the shepherd, and, falling on his knees, begged for mercy. The princess recognized her saviour at once, and did not need the proof of the dragon's teeth,

which he drew from his pocket. After
seeing the teeth, the king was convinced
that the shepherd was telling the truth.
The coachman was thrown into a
dungeon, and the shepherd took his place

at the princess's side. This time she did
not beg for the wedding to be put off, and
they all lived happily ever after.

The Unseen Bridegroom

By Joseph Jacobs

ONCE UPON A TIME there was a king and queen with three beautiful daughters. The most beautiful was the youngest, her name was Anima.

One day all three sisters were playing in the meadows, and Anima saw a bush with lovely flowers. As she pulled it up to plant in her own garden she plucked at the root, which gave way. Anima saw

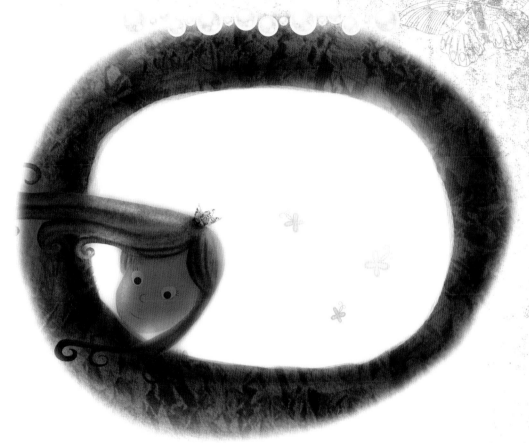

beneath it a stairway going down into
the earth. Being a brave girl, she crept
down the stairs for a long, long way,
until at last she came out into the open
air. Not far away, in front of her, she saw
a magnificent palace.

Anima ran towards it, and when she came to the magnificent gates, they opened without anybody being there. Anima went in and found it marvellously decorated. She came to a room with cosy couches, so she sat down.

Immediately a table appeared before her, with fruits and cakes and cool drinks upon it. So Anima took as much as she needed, fell asleep and did not awake until it was getting dark. She cried out, "Oh, I must go back to my father and mother, how shall I go? How shall I go?"

Then the soft voice of a young man spoke out and said, "Stay with me and be my bride, and you shall have all your heart desires."

But Anima cried out, "Let me see you!"

The voice replied, "That is forbidden. You must never look on my face, for my mother, the queen, has forbidden me to marry and laid a spell on me."

So sweet and gentle was his voice that Anima agreed to marry him, and they lived happily together, though he never came near her till all was dark, so that she could not see him. But after a time Anima became curious as to what manner of man her husband might be.

The next night when her husband came to Anima again, she waited until he was sleeping, then she lit the candle and looked at him. She was delighted to find that he was a most handsome man. But as she was looking at him three drops of wax fell upon his cheek. Then he woke up and knew that she had broken her promise.

"Oh, Anima," he said, "why have you done this? We must part until you can persuade my mother to break the spell."

With that came a rumbling of thunder and the flame of Anima's candle went out, the palace disappeared and she found herself on a bleak, bleak moor. She walked till she came to a house where an old woman greeted her and gave her something to eat and drink. Anima explained what had happened to her, and the old woman said, "I see. You have married my sister's son, and I fear she will never forgive you. If you go to her and ask for your husband, she'll give him up to you if you do all that she asks. Take this twig. If she asks what I think she will ask, strike it on the ground three times and help will come."

So Anima set out to find the queen. After a while she came to the palace of the queen — the mother of her invisible husband — and when she came into her presence she demanded to see him.

"What!" cried the queen, "how dare you marry my son!"

"It was his choice," said Anima, "and I am now his wife. Surely you will let me see him again."

"Well," said the queen, "First you must go into a barn where my stewards have poured together wheat, oats and rice into one great heap. If by nightfall you can separate them into three heaps perhaps, just perhaps, I may grant your request."

So Anima was led to the queen's great barn and left alone. Then she thought of the twig that the queen's sister had given her, and she struck it upon the ground.

Immediately, thousands of ants

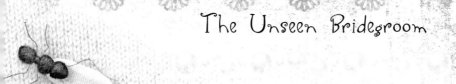

appeared and began to
separate the heap of grain,
taking the wheat to one corner,
the oats to another, and the
grains of rice to a third. By
nightfall all the grain had been
separated, and when the queen
came to let Anima out she
found the task had been
completed.

"You had help!" she cried.
"We'll see tomorrow if you
can do something all
by yourself."

The next day the queen summoned Anima, gave her a letter and said, "Take this to the Queen of the Underworld, and bring back what she will give you safely, and then I may let you see my son."

"How can I find her?" asked Anima.

"That you must find for yourself," the queen said, and left her.

Poor Anima did not know which way to go, but as she walked along the voice of someone invisible to her said softly, "Nearby, between two steep hills, is a deep valley. Go down the valley until you come to a deep river, and there you will see an old man ferrying people across the river. Put a coin between your teeth and let him take it from you, and he will carry you across, but speak not to him. Then, on the other side, you will come to a dark cave, and at the entrance is a savage dog. Give it a loaf of bread and it will let you pass. You will soon come to the Queen of the Underworld. Take what she gives you, but beware – do not eat or drink anything while you are there."

Anima recognized the voice of her husband and did all that he had told her. When she came before the Queen of the Underworld, the queen read the letter. Then she offered Anima cake and wine, but Amina refused, shaking her head, saying nothing. Then the Queen of the Underworld gave her a box and said she could leave.

Anima went back past the great dog and crossed the dark river. When she reached the castle again, she presented the box to the queen, who opened it and took out a wedding ring. Frowning, she said, "Someone has helped you but I cannot break my word. I suppose you must have my son."

As soon as she had said this Anima's husband appeared and took her into his arms, and they lived happily ever after.

The Sea-Hare

By the Brothers Grimm

ONCE UPON A TIME, there was a beautiful princess who lived in a grand palace. The palace had a tall tower with twelve windows that looked out in every direction. When she gazed through them, she could inspect her whole kingdom.

When she looked out of the first window, she could see more than any other human being, from the second she

could see still better, and so it went on,
until the twelfth, from which she saw
everything above the earth and under
the earth. Nothing at all could be
kept secret from her. She was proud,
and didn't want to share her
kingdom, so she declared that
no one would ever be her
husband unless he could hide

himself where she couldn't find him. Anyone who tried this, however, and was found, was to be locked up in a prison.

Ninety-seven men were already imprisoned in dungeons below the castle, and no one had come forward for a long time. The princess was delighted, and thought to herself, 'Now I shall be free as long as I live.'

Then three brothers came before her, and said that they wanted to try their luck. The eldest crept into a deep pit, but the princess saw him from the first window, made him come out and put him in prison. The second hid in the cellar of the palace, but she saw him also, and his fate was sealed. Then the youngest came and begged her to let him have three tries. As he was so handsome, and she liked the look of him, she said yes.

The youngest brother thought about how he should hide himself, but in vain. So he seized his gun and went out hunting. He saw a raven and was just going to fire, when the bird cried, "Don't shoot – I will make it worth your while."

The youth put his gun down, went on, and came to a lake. He saw a large fish, which had come up to the surface. When he had aimed at it, the fish cried, "Don't shoot, and I will reward you."

The youngest brother allowed it to dive down again, went onwards, and met a fox. He wanted to kill the fox and skin it, but the fox said, "Stop, and I will make it worth your while." The youth let it go, then returned home.

The next day the youngest brother was meant to hide himself, but he could not think where. He went into the forest to the raven and said, "Tell me where I can to hide myself, so that the king's daughter shall not see me." The raven thought it over for a long time. Then it fetched an egg from its nest, cut it into two, and shut the youth inside it. The raven then made it whole again, and seated itself on it.

When the king's daughter went to the first window she could not see the young man, nor could she from the other windows. But from the eleventh window she saw the egg moving slightly. She ordered the raven to be captured and the egg to be brought and broken, and the youth came out.

"If you can't do better than that," said the princess, "you've lost the challenge!"

The next day the youth went to the lake, called the fish and begged it to help him. So the fish swallowed him, and went down to the bottom of the lake.

The king's daughter looked through her windows, and even from the eleventh she could not see him. She was worried, but at last from the twelfth window she saw the bulge in the fish's stomach. She ordered the fish to be caught and squeezed, and then the youth appeared.

"Twice you are forgiven," said the princess, "but be sure — you will be locked up tomorrow."

On the last day, the young man went with a heavy heart, and met the fox.

"You are clever," said he, "where shall I hide myself so that the king's daughter cannot discover me?"

"That's hard," answered the fox, looking very thoughtful. But then it took the young man to a magic spring, dipped itself in it, and came out as a stall-keeper from the market. The youth then dipped himself in the water too, and changed into a sea-hare, a sea creature similar to a large slug.

The stall-keeper went into the town, and many people came to see the sea-hare. The princess came too and bought it. Before the stall-keeper handed over the sea-hare to the princess he whispered to it, "When the princess goes to the window, creep under the braids of her hair." And so he did. The princess went from window to window but could not see the young man. When she failed to spot him from the twelfth window, she was furious at being beaten.

She felt the sea-hare beneath her braids and threw it out of the window as far as she could. The sea-hare found the stall-keeper and they both hurried back to the spring. After they had changed back to their true forms they parted ways.

The youth returned to the princess and they were married, but he never told her where he had hidden himself for the third time, and who had helped him. The princess believed that the youth had done everything by himself, and she had a great respect for him, and they lived happily ever after.

The Swan Children of Lir

By Thomas Higginson

This is a story from Irish folklore. Erin is a name for Ireland. The name Aodh is pronounced 'Eh'.

KING LIR OF ERIN had four young children who were cared for by their stepmother, the new queen, but there came a time when she grew very jealous of the love their father had for them.

Sometimes there was murder in her heart, but she could not bear the thought of that wickedness, so she choose another way to rid herself of them.

One day she took them for a drive in her chariot. There was Princess Finola, who was eight years old, her three younger brothers — Aodh, Fiacre and little Conn, still a baby. They were beautiful children, with skin as white and soft as swans' feathers, and with large blue eyes and sweet voices. Reaching a lake, she told them that they might swim in the clear water, but as

soon as they were in it she struck them
with a fairy wand, and turned them into
four beautiful, snow-white swans — for
she was of the magician's race, and had

magical powers. The swans still had human voices, and Finola said to the queen, "This wicked deed of yours will be punished one day. How long shall we be in the shape of swans?"

"For three hundred years on smooth Lake Darvra," said the queen, "then three hundred years on the Sea of Moyle, and then three hundred years at Inis Glora, in the Great Western Sea. Until St Patrick comes to Ireland, and you hear the bell, you shall not be freed. Neither your power nor mine can now bring you back to human shape, but you shall keep your human reason and your speech, and you shall sing music so sweet that all who hear it shall listen."

She left them, and before long their
father, King Lir, came to the shore and
heard their singing. He asked how they
came to have human voices.

"We are your four children," said
Finola, "changed into swans by our
stepmother's jealousy."

"Then come and live with me," said
her sorrowing father.

"We are not permitted to leave the
lake," she said, "or live with our people
anymore. But we are allowed to dwell
together and to keep our reason and our
speech, and to sing sweet music to you."
So they sang to the king and his followers
and lulled them to sleep.

When King Lir awoke he determined to

find his wife, the queen. He discovered
she had returned to her father's palace
and so the king journeyed there.

When he arrived, King Lir told the
queen's father, King Bove, what the queen
had done, and he was furious.

"This wicked deed," said King Bove,
"shall punish the queen more than the
innocent children, for their suffering shall
end, but hers never shall."

King Bove asked the queen what bird,
beast or devil she most hated, and she
replied, "The demon of the
air − the bat."

"So be it," said King Bove, who also had magical power. He struck the queen with his wand, and she became a bat. Legend says 'She is still a demon of the air and shall be until the end of time'.

After this, people used to come to the lake and listen to the swans. The happy were made happier and the sad forgot their sorrows. There was peace in all that region, while war filled other lands. Vast changes took place in three centuries but still the swan-children lived and sang, until at the end of three hundred years they flew away to the stormy Sea of Moyle. From then on it was the law that no one should kill a swan in Erin.

Beside the Sea of Moyle they no longer

found the peaceful and
wooded shores they
had known, but
rocky coasts and wild
water. There came a
great storm one night,
and the swans knew that they could
not keep together. They resolved that if
separated they would meet at a rock
called Carricknarone. Finola arrived first,
and took her brothers under her wings. So
passed their lives until Finola sang one
day, "The Second Woe has passed – the

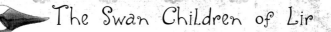

second period of
three hundred years."

They flew out on the ocean, and went
to the island of Inis Glora. There they
spent the next three hundred years amid
wilder storms and colder winds.

One May morning, as they floated in
the air around Inis Glora, they heard a
faint bell sounding across the eastern sea.
They saw beyond the waves, a priest,
with attendants around him on the Irish
shore. They knew that it must be St
Patrick. Sailing through the air towards
their native coast, they heard the bell
once more and they knew that all evil
spirits were fleeing. As they approached
the land, St Patrick stretched out his hand

and said, "Children of Lir, you may tread your native land again."

When they touched the shore, they became human again, but they now appeared old, pale and wrinkled.

And then they died, but, even as they did so, a change swiftly came over them. They were children again, in their white night-clothes, as when their father King Lir, long centuries ago, had kissed them at evening. Their time of sorrow was over, but the cruel stepmother remains in her bat-like shape, and a single glance at her little face will lead us to doubt whether she has repented of her evil deed.

The Princess and the Hare

A traditional German tale

THERE WAS ONCE A QUEEN who desperately wanted a child. She spoke to the Sun, and said, "Dear Sun, send me a little girl, and when she is twelve years old you may take her back."

So the Sun sent her a little girl, whom the queen called Letiko. She cared for her until she was twelve years old. Soon after,

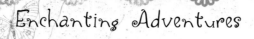

while Letiko was gathering herbs, the Sun came to her, and said, "Princess, tell your mother she must remember her promise."

Letiko went straight home and told her mother. When the queen heard, she shut all the doors and windows of the palace and stopped up all the chinks and holes, so that the Sun should not take her away. But she forgot to close up the keyhole, and

through it the Sun sent a ray into the house, which took hold of the little girl and carried her away to him. And there she lived with the Sun and did his work.

One day, the Sun sent Letiko to fetch straw. She sat down on the piles of straw and said, "As sighs this straw under my feet so sighs my heart for my mother."

This caused her to be so long away that the Sun asked her, when she came back, "Why have you been so long?"

She answered, "My slippers are too big, and I could not go faster."

So the Sun made the slippers smaller.

Another time he sent her to fetch water. At the spring she sat down and said, "As flows the water so flows my heart with longing for my mother."

She remained so long away that the Sun asked her why. And she answered, "My petticoat is too long and hinders me in walking."

So the Sun cut her petticoat shorter.

Another time, the Sun sent her to bring him a pair of sandals, and as the princess carried these in her hand she said, "As creaks the leather so creaks my heart after my little mother."

When she came home the Sun asked again, "Why do you come home so late?"

"My red hood is too wide, and it falls over my eyes."

Then he made the hood narrower.

At last, however, the Sun realized how

sad Letiko was. He sent her a second time to bring straw, and, slipping in after her, he heard how she cried for her mother. So, being not really bad-hearted, he went home, called two foxes to him, and said, "If you were to take Princess Letiko home what would you eat and drink if you should become hungry and thirsty on your journey?"

"We will eat her flesh and drink her blood."

When the Sun heard that, he told the foxes that they were not suitable. So he sent them away, and called two hares to him, and said, "If you were to take Princess Letiko home what would you eat and drink if you should become hungry and thirsty on your journey?"

"We will eat grass and drink from streams, of course."

"Then you may take her home," said the Sun.

So he said goodbye to Letiko and the hares set out with the princess. But because it was a long way to her home they became hungry. So they said to the little girl, "Climb this tree, dear Letiko, and stay there till we have finished eating some grass."

So Letiko climbed the tree, and the hares went grazing on grass. While they were eating, an evil snake-woman came to the tree and said, "Letiko, come down and see what beautiful shoes I have on.

If you will not come down I'll cut down the tree and eat you."

"Try it," said Letiko, "and then eat me."

So the snake-woman chopped with all her strength but she could not cut the tree down. When she realized this, she called, "Come down, I must feed my children."

"Go home and feed

163

them, and come back when you are ready," said Letiko.

When the snake-woman had gone Letiko called out, "Little hares! Little hares! Come here!"

They both ran back to her as fast as they could go. Then Letiko came down from the tree, and they went on their way. But the snake-woman was hurrying back to find them.

As Letiko drew near to the palace, the queen's dog recognized her, and called out happily, "Bow wow! Bow wow! Here is Letiko! My Queen, she is coming back to the palace!"

The queen said, "Hush! Will you make me burst with misery? I miss Letiko so much it breaks my heart!"

Next the queen's cat, which was lazing on the roof saw her, and called out, "Miaow! Miaow! Here comes Letiko!"

The queen said, "Keep silent!"

The nearer Letiko and the two hares came to the palace the nearer also came the snake-woman. The hares hustled Letiko into the back door of the palace. When the second hare was about to slip in too, the snake-woman caught it by its little tail and tore it off.

As the second hare came in, the queen stood up and said, "Welcome, dear little hare. Because you have brought back my daughter Letiko I will give you a beautiful silver tail."

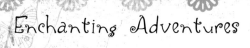

And she did so, and lived happily ever
after with her daughter, Letiko.

Kate Crackernuts

A traditional Scottish fairy tale

A henwife is an old word for
a wise woman or witch.

NCE UPON A TIME there was a
king and a queen. The king had
a daughter named Anne, and
the queen had a daughter named Kate.
Anne was far bonnier than Kate, but
they loved one another like real sisters.
The queen was jealous that the king's

daughter was prettier than her own, so she decided to try and spoil her beauty. She took advice from the henwife, who told her to send the lassie to her the next morning before she ate anything.

Early next morning, the queen said to Anne, "Go, my dear, to the henwife in the glen, and ask her for some eggs."

Anne set out, but as she passed through the kitchen she saw a crust, and ate it.

When she came to the henwife she asked for eggs, as she had been told to do. The henwife had laid a spell on her pot, and said to Anne, "Lift the lid off that pot there and see." The lassie did so, but nothing happened. "Go home to your mammie and tell her to keep her larder locked," said the henwife.

So she went home to the queen and told her what the henwife had said. The queen knew from this that the lassie had eaten something, so she watched her the next morning and sent her away with nothing to eat. The princess saw some country-folk picking peas by the roadside, however, and being very kind she spoke to them. They gave her a handful of the peas, which she ate as she walked.

When she came to the henwife, she was told again, "Lift the lid off the pot and you'll see."

So Anne lifted the lid but nothing happened. The henwife angrily said to Anne, "Tell your mammie the pot won't boil if the fire's away."

So Anne went home and told the queen what she had said.

On the third day the queen went along with the girl to the henwife. This time, when Anne lifted the lid off the pot, off fell her own pretty head, and on jumped a sheep's head.

So the queen was now quite satisfied. When they got back to the palace, however, Kate, felt so sorry for her sister. She took a fine linen cloth and wrapped it around Anne. She took her by the hand and they both went out into the world to seek their fortune.

They went on, and on, and on, until they came to a castle. Kate knocked at the door and asked for a night's lodging for herself and a sick sister. They went in and found it was a king's castle, who had two sons. One son was very sick and no one could find out what was wrong. The curious thing was that whoever watched him at night was never seen again. So the king had offered a sack of silver to anyone who would sit up with him. Now Kate was a very brave girl, so she offered to try and help.

Up until midnight all went well. As twelve o'clock rung, however, the sick prince rose, dressed himself, and slipped downstairs. Kate followed, but he didn't seem to notice her. The prince went to the stable and saddled his horse. He called his hound then jumped into the saddle – and Kate leapt lightly up behind him.

Away rode the prince and Kate through the green wood. Kate, as they rode, plucked nuts from the trees and filled her apron with them. They rode on and on until they came to a green hill. The prince stopped the horse and spoke,

Kate Crackernuts

"Open, green hill,
and let the young prince
in with his horse and his
hound," and Kate
added, "and his lady
him behind."

Immediately an opening
appeared in the green hill,
and they went in.

The prince entered a
magnificent hall, brightly lit.
Then many beautiful fairies
surrounded the prince and
led him off to dance.

Meanwhile Kate, without being noticed, hid herself behind the door. There she saw the prince dancing and dancing and dancing.

At last the cockerel crew, and the prince made haste to get on horseback. Kate jumped up behind and home they rode.

When the morning sun rose they came in and found Kate sitting down by the fire and cracking her nuts.

The second night passed as the first had done. The prince got up at midnight and rode away to the green hill and the fairy ball, and Kate went with him. This time she did not watch the prince, for she knew he would be dancing. She saw a fairy baby playing with a wand, and

overheard one of
the fairies say,
"Three strokes
of that wand
would make
Kate's sick sister as
bonnie as ever she was."
So Kate rolled nuts to the
fairy baby, who toddled
after them, letting the wand
fall. Then Kate took up the
wand and put it in her apron.
When the cockerel crew they rode
home as before, and the moment Kate
got home to her room she rushed to find
Anne. She tapped her with the wand
three times, and the nasty sheep's head

fell off and she was her own pretty self
again. On the third night Kate agreed to
watch again, but only if she could marry
the sick prince. Everything happened as
before, but this time the fairy baby was
playing with an apple. Kate heard one of
the fairies say, "A bite of that apple would
make the sick prince as well as ever he
was." So Kate rolled all the nuts to the
fairy baby until the apple was dropped,
and Kate put it in her apron.

As the cockerel crew they set off again,
but instead of cracking her nuts as she
used to, Kate cut up the apple.

"Oh!" said the sick prince, "I wish I
could have a bite of that apple."

Kate gave him a bite of the apple, and

he rose up quite well, dressed himself, and sat down by the fire, and when the folk came in next morning they found Kate and the young prince cracking nuts and talking happily together.

So Kate and the prince were married in a grand ceremony, as she had wished. Meanwhile, the young prince's brother had fallen in love with Kate's sister, Anne. They too were married and both couples lived happily ever after.

Earl Mar's Daughter

By Joseph Jacobs

ONE FINE SUMMER'S DAY, Earl Mar's daughter went into the castle grounds. As she strolled through the gardens she would stop from time to time to listen to the music of the birds. After a while she rested, and sat in the shade of a green oak tree. She looked up and saw a dove sitting high up on one of its branches. Earl Mar's daughter said, "Coo-my-dove, my dear, come down to

me and I will give you a
golden cage. I'll take you
home and look after
you well."

As she said these words the dove flew
down from the branch and settled on her
shoulder, nestling
up against her
neck while she smoothed
its feathers. Then she took
it home to her room.

The day was done and
the night came on and Earl
Mar's daughter was thinking
of going to sleep when,
turning round, she found at
her side a handsome

young man. She was startled, for the door had been locked for hours. But she was a brave girl and said, "What are you doing here, young man?"

"Hush! Hush!" the young man whispered. "I was the cooing dove that you coaxed down from the tree."

"But who are you?" she said quietly, "and how did you come to be changed into that dear little bird?"

"My name is Florentine, and my mother is a queen — something more than a queen — for she knows magic. I would not do as she wished, so she turned me into a dove by day, but at night her spells lose their power and I become a man again. Today I crossed the sea and saw you for the first time. I was glad to be a bird, so that I could come near you. Unless you love me, I'll never be happy."

"But if I love you," said she, "will you not fly away and leave me one of these fine days?"

"Never, never," said the prince "be my wife and I'll be yours forever. By day a bird, by night a prince, I will always be by your side as a husband, dear."

So they were married in secret and lived happily in the castle and no one knew that every night Coo-my-dove became Prince Florentine.

Seven years passed and then a great trouble came to them. Earl Mar wished to marry his daughter to a fine man who

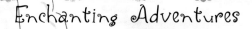

came wooing her. Her
father insisted but she
said, "Father dear, I do
not wish to marry, I can be quite happy
with Coo-my-dove here."

Then her father flew into a mighty
rage and said, "Tomorrow, so sure as I
live, I'll twist that bird's neck," and he
stamped out of her room.

"Oh no!" said Coo-my-dove,
"It's time that I was away," and
so he jumped upon the window
sill and in a moment was
flying away.

And he flew and he flew
over the deep, deep sea, till he
came to his mother's castle.

The queen, his mother, was taking a walk when she saw the pretty dove flying overhead and alighting on the castle walls.

"Here dancers, come and dance your jigs," she called, "and pipers, pipe you well, for here's my own Florentine, come back to me to stay."

"No, mother," said Florentine, "no dancers for me and no minstrels, for my dear wife is to be wed tomorrow, and sad is the day for me."

"What can I do, my son?" said the queen, "tell me, and it shall be done if my magic has power to do it."

"Well then, mother dear, turn the twenty-four dancers into twenty-four grey herons, and let my pipers become seven white swans, and let me be a hawk and their leader."

"Alas my son," she said, "my magic is not strong enough. But perhaps the witch-wife of Ostree, may know better."

And away she hurried to the witch-wife's cave to speak to her. After a while the queen came out, muttering over some burning herbs. Suddenly Coo-my-dove changed into a goshawk and around him flew twenty-four grey herons and above them flew seven swans.

Without a word or a goodbye off they flew over the deep blue sea. They flew and they flew until they swooped down on Earl Mar's castle just as the wedding party were setting out for the church.

First came the men-at-arms and then the bridegroom's friends. Then came Earl Mar's men, followed by the bridegroom. And lastly, pale and beautiful, Earl Mar's daughter herself. They moved slowly until they came past the trees on which the birds were settling. A word from Prince Florentine, the hawk, and they all rose into the air, herons beneath, swans above, and hawk circling above all. The wedding guests wondered at the sight when, swoop! The herons were down among them scattering the men-at-arms.

The swans took the bride while the hawk dashed down and tied the bridegroom to a tree. Then the herons

gathered themselves into one feather bed.
The swans placed the princess upon them,
and suddenly they all rose in the air

bearing the bride away with them in safety towards Prince Florentine's home.

Surely a wedding party was never so disturbed in this world! What could they do? They watched the pretty bride be carried away until she and all the birds disappeared. That very day Prince Florentine brought Earl Mar's daughter to his mother's castle. She took the spell off him and they lived happily ever after.

The Twelve Dancing Princesses

By the Brothers Grimm

ONCE UPON A TIME there was a king who had twelve daughters, each one more beautiful than the other. Their beds were all together in one room, and when they went to bed, their door was locked and barred. But the next morning their shoes were always danced to pieces, and no one knew where they had been or how it had happened. The king proclaimed that whoever could discover where the princesses went dancing each night could choose one of them for his wife and become king after his death.

Now it happened that a poor soldier, who because of his wounds could no longer serve in the army, was making his way to the city where the king lived. He met an old woman who asked him where he was going. "I'm not sure myself," he said. "But I would like to become king and discover where the princesses are dancing their shoes to pieces."

"Oh," said the old woman, "that isn't so difficult. Just do not drink the wine that one of them will bring you in the evening." Then she gave him a cloak and said, "Put this on, and you will be invisible, and you can follow them."

Having received this good advice, the soldier went to the king, and announced himself as a suitor. He was well received, and was given royal clothes to wear.

That evening at bedtime he was escorted to a bedchamber outside the princesses' room. Just as he was going to bed, the eldest princess brought him a goblet of wine, but he secretly poured it away. He lay down, and after a little while began to snore as if he were in the deepest sleep. The twelve princesses heard him and laughed.

Then they got up, opened their wardrobes, chests, and closets, took out their best clothes, and made themselves beautiful in front of their mirrors.

When they were ready, they approached the soldier, but he did not move at all as he feigned sleep. As soon as they thought it was safe, the eldest princess went to her bed and knocked on it. It immediately sank beneath the floor, revealing a trapdoor. The soldier watched how they all climbed down, one after the other, the eldest leading the way. When the youngest princess had gone through, he jumped up, put on the cloak, and followed her. But halfway down the stairs he accidentally stepped on her dress. Frightened, she called out, "It's not right! Something is holding my dress."

"Don't be so simple," said the eldest princess. "You have just caught yourself on a hook."

Then they passed through three walkways lined with trees made from gold, then silver, then clear diamond. The soldier broke a twig from each. The cracking sound frightened the youngest princess each time, but the eldest princess insisted that it was only the sounds of joyful salutes.

They continued until they came to a large lake. Twelve boats were there, and in each boat there was a handsome prince waiting for them. Each prince took a princess into his boat. The soldier snuck into the boat of the youngest princess, and her prince said, "I am as strong as ever, but the boat seems to be much heavier. I am rowing as hard as I can."

"It must be the warm weather," said the youngest princess. "It's far too hot for me as well."

On the other side of the water there was a beautiful, brightly illuminated castle. Joyful music, kettle drums, and trumpets sounded forth. They rowed over and went inside.

Each handsome prince danced with his princess. The soldier danced along as well, and when a princess held up a goblet of wine, he drank it empty as she lifted it to her mouth. This frightened the youngest princess, but the eldest silenced her every time. They danced there until three o'clock the next morning, when their shoes were danced to pieces.

The princes rowed them back across the water. When they were on the steps, the soldier ran ahead and got into bed so that when the twelve tired princesses came in he was again snoring loudly.

"He will be no risk to us," they said. Then they took off their beautiful clothes, put them away, placed their worn out shoes under their beds and went to sleep.

The next morning the soldier said nothing, for he wanted to see the amazing thing again. He went along the second and third nights, and everything happened as before. Each time they danced until their shoes were in pieces. The third time he also took a goblet as a piece of evidence.

The hour came when he was to give his answer. He brought the three twigs and the goblet with him. The twelve princesses stood behind the door and listened to what he had to say. The king asked, "Where did my daughters dance their shoes to pieces?"

He answered, "In an underground

castle with twelve princes." Then he told the whole story and brought forth the pieces of evidence. When the princesses saw that they had been found out, and that their denials did no good, they admitted everything. Then the king asked the soldier which princess he would like for a wife.

He answered, "I myself am no longer young, so I'd like to marry the eldest princess."

Their wedding was held the same day, and the kingdom was promised to him following the king's death.

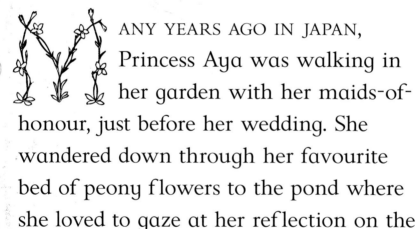

Princess Peony

By Richard Gordon Smith

ANY YEARS AGO IN JAPAN, Princess Aya was walking in her garden with her maids-of-honour, just before her wedding. She wandered down through her favourite bed of peony flowers to the pond where she loved to gaze at her reflection on the nights of the full moon.

When she was near the pond her foot slipped, and she would have fallen into

the water had it not been that
a young man appeared as
if by magic and caught her.
She saw him briefly across
the water, then he disappeared.

199

The maids-of-honour had seen her slip and a glimmer of light but that was all. But Princess Aya had seen more. She had seen the most handsome young man she could imagine.

"Twenty-one years old," she said to her favourite maid, "he must have been a samurai of the highest order. His dress was covered with my favourite peonies. If only I could have seen him a minute longer, to thank him for saving me! Who can he be? And how could he have got into the palace gardens, through all the guards?"

After that evening Princess Aya fell sick. She could not eat or sleep, and turned pale. The wedding day came and went without the event — she was far too sick for that. As a last resource, her father sent for her favourite maid and demanded to know if she could give any reason for his daughter's mysterious sickness. Had she a secret lover? Had she a particular dislike for her husband-to-be?

Her maid told him about the mysterious samurai. "Since that evening," she said, "our beloved Princess Aya has been sick, Sir. It is sickness of the heart. She is deeply in love with the young samurai she saw. There never was such a handsome man in the world before."

That evening the poor princess was more wearily unhappy than ever before.

Thinking to enliven her a little, the maids sent for a celebrated musician. The weather being hot, they were sitting on the balcony, and while the musician was playing, there appeared suddenly, from behind the peonies, the same handsome young samurai. He was visible to all this time — even the peonies embroidered on his clothes.

"There he is! There he is!" cried the maids, at which he instantly disappeared again. The princess seemed more lively than she had been for days.

Next night, while two of the maids were playing music for their mistress, the figure of the young man appeared and disappeared once more. A thorough search was made in the immense peony flowerbeds with absolutely no result, not even the sign of a footprint.

A meeting was held, and it was decided by Princess Aya's father that a veteran officer of great strength and renown, Maki Hiogo, should try to capture the youth, should he appear again that evening. He arrived dressed in black to make him invisible in the dark night and hid himself among the peonies.

Music seemed to fascinate the young samurai. It was while music was being played that he had made his appearances. As the ladies played a piece called 'Sofuren', there, sure enough, arose the figure of a young samurai, dressed magnificently in clothes, which were covered with embroidered peonies.

Maki Hiogo stealthily approached the young man, and, seizing him around the waist, held him tight. But after a few seconds Maki Hiogo felt a kind of wet steam falling on his face. Still grasping the young samurai — for he had made up his mind that he would secure him — he fell to the ground.

As the guards rushed over to help, Maki Hiogo shouted, "Come, gentlemen! I have caught him. Come and see!" But the man had disappeared, he only held a large peony in his arms!

By this time the king had arrived at the spot where Maki Hiogo lay, and so had

Princess Aya and her maids-in-waiting.

All were astounded and mystified except the king himself, who said "Ah! It is as I thought. It is the spirit of the peony flower that took the form of a prince."

Turning to his daughter and her maids, he said, "You must take this as a great compliment, and pay respect to the peony. Show the one caught by Maki Hiogo kindness by taking care of it."

So Princess Aya carried the flower back to her room, where she put it in a vase of water and placed it near her pillow. She felt as if she had her sweetheart with her.

Day by day she got better. She tended the peony herself, and, strangely, the flower seemed to get stronger and stronger, instead of fading. At last the princess recovered. She became radiantly beautiful once again, while the peony continued to remain in perfect bloom, showing no sign of dying.

As Princess Aya was now perfectly well again, her father could no longer put off the wedding. Some days later, the bridegroom and all his family arrived at the castle, and the next day he was married to Princess Aya in a great ceremony.

As soon as the wedding was over, the peony was found dead and withered still in its vase. After this, the villagers always called Princess Aya 'Princess Peony' instead.

Noel's Princess

An extract from
The Story of the Treasure Seekers
by E Nesbit

S HE HAPPENED QUITE ACCIDENTALLY.
We were not looking for a
princess at all just then, but Noel
had said he was going to find a princess
all by himself — and he really did.

Greenwich Park is a jolly good place to
play in, especially the parts that aren't
near Greenwich. I often wish the park
was nearer our house, but I suppose a

park is a difficult thing to move.

The day the princess happened was a fine, hot day, last October, and we were quite tired with the walk up to the park.

When we'd rested a little, Alice said, "I see the white witch bear among the trees! Let's track it and slay it in its lair."

"I am the bear," said Noel, so he crept away, and we followed him among the trees. Often the witch bear was out of sight, and you didn't know where it would jump out from. Sometimes it just followed.

We hunted the bear in and out of the trees, and then we lost him altogether. Suddenly we found the wall of the park. Noel wasn't anywhere about. There was a door in the wall and it was open, so we went through.

We went over the stones on tiptoes, and found another wall with another door on the other side. We went through that too, on tiptoes. It really was an adventure.

There was Noel. He was standing looking at a little girl — she was the funniest little girl you ever saw.

She was like a doll, with a pale face, and long yellow hair done up in two pigtails. Her cheeks came high up, like little shelves under her eyes. Her eyes were small and blue. She had on a funny black frock. As we came up we heard her say to Noel, "Who are you?"

"I'm Prince Camaralzaman."

The funny little girl looked pleased.

"I thought at first you were a common boy," she said. Then she saw the rest of us and said, "Are you princesses and princes too?"

Of course we said, "Yes," and she said, "I am a princess also." She said it very well too, exactly as if it were true. We were very glad, because it is so seldom you meet any children who can begin to play right off without having everything explained to them.

The little girl had a funny voice — she didn't talk at all like we do.

Then we asked her name, and she went on and on, I thought she would never stop. The first were Pauline, Alexandra, Alice, and Mary was one, and Victoria, for we all heard that, and it ended with Hildegarde Cunigonde something or other, princess of something else.

When she'd done, Horace Octavius said, "That's jolly good! Say it again!" and she did. We told her our names, but she thought they were too short, so when it was Noel's turn he said he was Prince Noel Camaralzaman Ivan Constantine Charlemagne James John Edward Biggs Maximilian Bastable Prince of

Lewisham, but when she asked him to say it again of course he could only get the first two names right, because he'd made it up as he went on.

So the princess said, "You are old enough to know your own name." She was very grave and serious.

The little girl asked us where our maids and governesses were and we told her we hadn't any.

"How nice! Did you come here alone?"

"Yes," said Dora, "we came from across the heath."

"You are fortunate," said the little girl. "I should like to go on the heath. There are donkeys there. I should like to ride them. My governess will not permit it."

"Never mind," said Noel, "I've got a lot of money. Come and have a ride now." But the little girl shook her head and said she was afraid it would not be correct.

Then we showed her how to play cross-touch, and puss in the corner, and

tag. She began to laugh at last and looked less like a doll.

She was running after Dicky when suddenly she stopped short and looked as if she was going to cry. And we looked too, and there were two prim ladies with little mouths and tight hair. One of them said in quite an awful voice, "Pauline, who are these children?"

The little girl said we were princes and princesses — which was silly, to a grown-up person.

The gruff lady gave a short, horrid laugh, and said, "Princes, indeed! They're only common children!"

The little girl cried out, "Oh, I am so glad! When I am grown-up I'll always play with common children."

And she ran at us, and began to kiss us one by one, when the horrid lady said, "Your Highness go indoors at once!"

The little girl answered, "I won't!"

Then the prim lady said, "Wilson, carry her Highness indoors."

The little girl was carried away screaming, and between her screams she shrieked, "Common children! I am glad!"

The nasty lady then remarked to us, "Now go at once, or I will have to send for the police!"

So we all came away very quickly, and when we got outside Dora said, "So she was really a princess."

"And I thought it was play. And it was

real. I wish I'd known! I should have liked to ask her lots of things," said Alice.

Horace Octavius said he would have liked to ask her what she had for dinner and whether she had a crown.

So we all went home across the heath, and made toast for tea. When we were eating it Noel said, "I wish I could give her some toast."

He sighed as he said it, so we knew he was thinking of the princess. He says now that she was as beautiful as the day, but we remember her quite well, and she was nothing of the kind.

Gallant Girls and Brave Lasses

Admetus and Alcestis

By James Baldwin

HE KING OF IOLCUS was a cruel tyrant named Pelias, who cared for nobody but himself. Pelias had a daughter named Alcestis, who was as fair as a rose in June and so gentle and good that everybody praised her. Many a prince from over the sea had come to woo Alcestis but there was only one to whom she would listen – her young neighbour, King Admetus.

So Admetus went before gruff King Pelias to ask him whether he might marry the beautiful Alcestis.

"If you want her," said the cruel king "you must come for her in a chariot drawn by a lion and a wild boar." And Pelias laughed, and drove the young man out of his palace.

Admetus went away feeling very sad, for who had ever heard of harnessing a lion and a wild boar together in a chariot? The bravest man in the world could not do such a thing as that.

Early the next morning he built an altar of stones in the open field and lifted his hands towards the mountain tops and called to the god Apollo.

"Lord of the Silver Bow," he cried, "if ever I have shown kindness to the poor and the distressed, come now and help me, for I am in sore need."

Hardly was he done speaking when the bright god Apollo came down and stood before him.

"Kindest of kings," he said, "tell me how I can help you."

Then Admetus told him all about the fair Alcestis, and the condition her father had made.

"Come with me," said Apollo, "and I will help you."

Then the two went together into the forest, Apollo leading the way. Soon they chased a lion from its lair and the quick-footed Apollo seized the beast by its mane, and although it howled and snapped with its fierce jaws he slipped a bridle upon it. Then Admetus scared a wild boar from a thicket.

When Apollo had caught that too, he went on through the forest, leading the two beasts, one with his right hand, the other with his left. A golden chariot stood by the roadside as if waiting for them, and the lion and the boar were soon harnessed to it. It was a strange team, and the two beasts tried hard to fight each other, but Apollo lashed them with a whip until they lost their fierceness.

Admetus climbed into the chariot, Apollo stood by his side and held the reins and drove into Iolcus.

Old King Pelias was astonished when he saw the wonderful chariot and the glorious charioteer, and when Admetus again asked him for the Princess Alcestis, he could not refuse. And so Admetus and Alcestis were married, and everybody except gruff King Pelias was glad. Apollo himself was a guest at the

wedding feast, and he brought a present for the young bridegroom, it was a promise from the Mighty Folk upon the mountain top that if Admetus should ever be sick and in danger of death, he might become well again if someone who loved him would die for him.

Admetus and Alcestis lived together happily for a long time, and all the people in their little kingdom loved and blessed them. But at last Admetus fell sick, and, as he grew worse, all feared he would die. Then those who loved him remembered the wedding gift that Apollo had given him, and they began to ask who would be willing to die for him.

His brothers and sisters were asked if

they would die for Admetus, but they turned away. There were men in the town whom he had befriended and who owed their lives to him, but they too refused to help.

Now, while everyone was shaking their heads and saying, "Not I," Alcestis went into her room and called to Apollo. She asked if she might give up her life to save her husband. Then without a thought of fear she lay down upon her bed and closed her eyes, and when her maidens came into the room they found her dead.

At the very same time Admetus felt his sickness leave him, and he sprang up as well and strong as he had ever been. He made haste to find his beloved Alcestis and tell her the good news. But when he went into her room, he found her lying lifeless on her couch, and knew at once that she had died for him. His grief was so great that he could not speak, and he wished that death had taken him instead.

Throughout the land every eye was wet with weeping for Alcestis. Admetus sat by the couch where his young queen lay, and held her cold hand in his own. All through the dark hours he sat there alone. The morning dawned, but he did not want to see the light.

At last the sun began to rise in the east, and then Admetus was surprised to feel the hand which he held growing warm. He saw a pink tinge coming into the pale cheeks of Alcestis. A moment later she opened her eyes and sat up, alive and well. As Admetus held Alcestis' hand, he told her he was overjoyed to be reunited with her again.

When Alcestis had died, the Shadow

Leader led her to Proserpine, the queen of the Underworld.

"Who is this who comes so willingly?" asked the pale-faced queen.

And when she was told how Alcestis had given her life to save her husband, she was moved with pity. Proserpine told the Shadow Leader take Alcestis back to the sunlight of the Upperworld.

So Alcestis came back to life, and for many years she and Admetus lived in their kingdom. At last, when they were both very old, the Shadow Leader led them both away together.

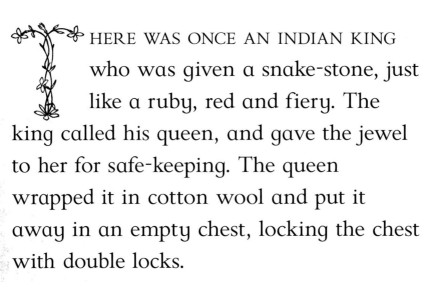

The Ruby Prince

By Flora Annie Steel

HERE WAS ONCE AN INDIAN KING who was given a snake-stone, just like a ruby, red and fiery. The king called his queen, and gave the jewel to her for safe-keeping. The queen wrapped it in cotton wool and put it away in an empty chest, locking the chest with double locks.

So there the ruby snake-stone lay for

twelve long years. At the end of that time the king sent for his queen, and said, "Bring me the ruby, I wish to satisfy myself that it is safe."

The queen told her servant to bring the box, and they unlocked the chest. To everybody's astonishment out stepped a handsome young man.

"Who are you?" said the king, "and where is my jewel?"

"I am the Ruby Prince," said the man, "More than that you cannot know."

The king had a fair daughter, who fell in love with the young man. They were married in great state, and half the kingdom was given to them to rule.

But the young bride, as much as she

loved her handsome husband, was sad because she didn't know who he was. The other women in the palace teased her for marrying a stranger.

So day after day, she would ask her husband to tell her who he was, and every day the Ruby Prince would reply, "Dear heart, that you must not know!"

Yet still the princess begged and wept, until one day when they were standing by the riverside, she whispered, "If you love me, tell me where you come from!"

Now the Ruby Prince's foot touched the water as he replied, "Dear heart, that you must not know!"

But the princess said again, "If you love me, tell me where you are from!"

The Ruby Prince stood knee-deep in the water. His face was sad as he replied, "Dear heart, that you must not know!"

Again the bride asked her question. By now the Ruby Prince was waist-deep in the stream.

"Dear heart, anything but that!" He cried.

"Tell me!" cried the princess, and as she spoke, a jewelled snake wearing a crown reared out of the water. It had a ruby in the middle of its forehead. Then with a sorrowful look, the snake disappeared beneath the surface.

Then the princess went home and wept bitterly, cursing her own curiosity. She wished she hadn't asked her husband to tell her where he had come from. The princess offered a reward of a bushel of gold to anyone who could bring her any information about her husband.

At last a dancing-woman, came to the princess, and said, "Last night I saw a strange thing. When I was out gathering sticks, I lay down to rest under a tree, and fell asleep. When I awoke it was light, but neither daylight nor moonlight. While I wondered, a sweeper came out from a snake-hole at the foot of the tree, and swept the ground with his broom. Then followed two carpet-bearers, who spread costly rugs, and then disappeared. Then I heard music, and from the snake-hole came a procession of young men, glittering with jewels, and the middle one seemed to be the king. Then while the musicians played, one by one the young men rose and danced before the king. But one, who wore a red ruby on his forehead, danced poorly and looked pale and sad.

So the next night the princess went with the dancing-girl to the tree, where they hid and waited to see what might happen. Sure enough, after a while it became light that was neither sunlight nor moonlight. Then just as the dancing-woman had described, the glittering procession swept out. How the princess's heart ached when she recognized her dearest husband, and saw how pale he had become.

When all had performed before the king, the light faded, and the princess crept home. Every night she would go to the tree and watch, but all day she would weep, because she seemed no nearer to getting her husband back.

Then one day the dancing-girl came to the princess and said, "O princess, I think I have hit upon a plan. The snake-king is passionately fond of dancing, and yet it is only men who dance before him. Now, what if a woman were to dance in front of him instead? He might be so pleased that he would grant her anything she asked for?"

So the princess learnt to dance, and in an incredibly short time she was far better than her teacher. Never before or since was such a graceful, charming, elegant dancer seen. Everything about her was perfection. Then she dressed herself the finest jewelled muslins and brocades, till she shone and sparkled like a star.

That night, with a fast-beating heart she nervously hid behind the tree and waited. When they appeared, as before, the Ruby Prince looked paler and sadder than ever, and when his turn came to dance, he hesitated, as if sick at heart.

But from bchind the tree stepped the

princess, and she danced marvellously before the king. Never before was there such a dance! Everybody held their breath till it was done, and then the king cried aloud, "O unknown dancer, ask for

whatever you like, and it shall be yours!"

"Please give me the man who looks so sad, for that is why I danced!" replied the princess at once.

The snake-king looked very fierce, and his eyes glittered as he said, "I should kill you were it not for my promise. Take him, and be gone!"

Quick as a thought, the princess seized the Ruby Prince by the hand, dragged him beyond the circle, and fled.

After that they lived very happily. The princess held her tongue and never again asked her husband where he came from.

Tatterhood

By George Webbe Dasent

ONCE UPON A TIME there was a king and queen who had two baby princesses. The first to be born had a wooden spoon in her hand, and rode upon a goat.

"If I'm your mamma," said the queen, "Then God give me grace to do better next time."

"Oh, don't be sorry," said the girl, who

rode on the goat, "for one will soon come after me who is better looking."

After a while the queen had another girl, who was so fair and sweet, no one had ever set eyes on such a lovely child. They called the eldest Tatterhood, because she was always so plain and ragged, and because she wore a hood that hung about her ears in tatters.

One Christmas Eve, when the princesses were grown-up, there rose a frightful noise outside the queen's chamber. Tatterhood asked what it was that crashed so loudly.

The queen told her that a pack of witches had turned up. So Tatterhood said she would go out and drive them away.

She begged the queen to be mindful and
keep all the doors closed. Having said
this, off she went with her wooden spoon.
She began to hunt and sweep away the
hags. While this was happening there
was such a loud noise in the passage.

Now, exactly what happened next I'm
sure I can't tell, but Tatterhood's sister had
just peeped out to see how things were
going when POP, up came an old
witch, who whisked her out of
the window. When
Tatterhood came back
and found her
sister gone,
she scolded
everyone

nearby for not taking better care.

"I'll see if I can set her free," she said.

She asked the king for a boat but no captain or sailors. She would sail away all alone. As there was no stopping her, at last they let her have her own way. So Tatterhood sailed off, and steered her boat

to where the witches lived. When she came to the landing-place, she rode on her goat up to the witches' castle. Tatterhood saw her sister weeping through an open window, so she leapt on her goat, jumped inside, snatched up her sister, and they set off.

The witches came after her, to trying to get the princess back again. They flocked about her as thick as a swarm of bees. But the goat snorted and butted with his horns, and Tatterhood beat and banged them with her wooden spoon, and the pack of witches had to give up.

They set off for home but the winds blew strongly and their boat was blown into a strange land. The king of that land had two sons. When he saw the strange sail, he sent messengers down to the beach to find out where it came from, and who owned it. When the king's men arrived there, they saw not a living soul on board but Tatterhood, and there she was, riding round and round the deck on her goat at full speed, till her straggly hair streamed in the wind. The folk from the palace were all amazed, and asked if there was anyone else on board?

"Yes," said Tatterhood, "my sister."

They wanted to see her but Tatterhood said, "No one shall see her, unless the king comes himself."

When the servants got back to the palace and told what they had seen, the king and his sons set out at once. When they got there, Tatterhood led out her fair sister. The king's eldest son fell in love straight away and asked to marry her. Tatterhood said he couldn't, unless the youngest son chose to marry Tatterhood as well. The younger prince wasn't keen, but at last the king talked him round.

When all was ready, they were to go to church. The younger prince thought it was the saddest day of his life. First, the older prince drove off with his bride, and she was so lovely that all the people stopped to look at her. Next came the sorrowful younger prince on horseback by the side of Tatterhood, who trotted along on her goat with her wooden spoon.

"Why don't you talk?" asked Tatterhood.

"What should I talk about?" answered the youngest prince.

"Well, you might at least ask me why I ride upon this ugly goat," said Tatterhood.

"Why do you ride on that ugly goat?" asked the prince.

"Is it an ugly goat? Why, it's the grandest horse a bride ever rode on," answered Tatterhood, and in a trice the goat became the finest horse the prince had ever seen.

Then they rode on again, but the prince

didn't say a word. So Tatterhood asked him again why he didn't talk, and said, "You can at least ask me why I ride with this ugly spoon in my fist."

"Why do you ride with that ugly spoon?" asked the prince.

"Is it an ugly spoon? Why, it's the loveliest silver wand a bride ever bore," said Tatterhood, and in a trice it became a silver wand, so dazzling bright, that sunbeams glistened from it.

So they rode on a bit further, but the prince was just as sorrowful, and never said a word. In a little while, Tatterhood told him to ask why she wore the ugly grey hood. So he asked and she said, "Is it an ugly hood? Why, it's the brightest golden crown a bride ever wore." And it became a crown on the spot.

Now, they rode on a long while again, and the prince was so woeful, that he sat without sound or speech just as before. So his bride asked him again why he didn't talk, and told him to ask, why her face was so ugly and ashen-grey?

"Ah!" asked the prince, "why is your face so ugly and ashen-grey?"

"I, ugly?" said the bride. "You think my sister pretty, but I am ten times prettier." And lo, when the prince looked at her, she was so lovely, he thought there was never so lovely a woman in all the world. After that, I shouldn't wonder if the prince found his tongue, and no longer rode along with his head hanging down.

So they drank from the bridal cup both deep and long, and after that both princes set out with their brides to the princesses' father's palace, and there they had another feast. And, if you make haste and run, I dare say you'll find there's still a drop of the bridal ale left for you.

Maid Maleen

By the Brothers Grimm

THERE WAS ONCE A PRINCESS called Maid Maleen, who was very beautiful. She fell in love with a handsome prince but her father wished her to marry another man, so the prince was sent away. However, Maid Maleen said to her father, "I will take no other husband but him."

Then the king flew into a fury, and

ordered a dark tower to be built, into which no ray of sunlight should enter. When it was finished, he said, "Here you shall be imprisoned for seven years, and then I will come and see if you will agree." Food and drink for the seven years was carried into the tower, and then she was led into it and walled up, and cut off from the world.

There she sat in the darkness, and knew not when day or night began. The time passed, and when the supply of food and drink grew small she knew that the seven years were coming to an end.

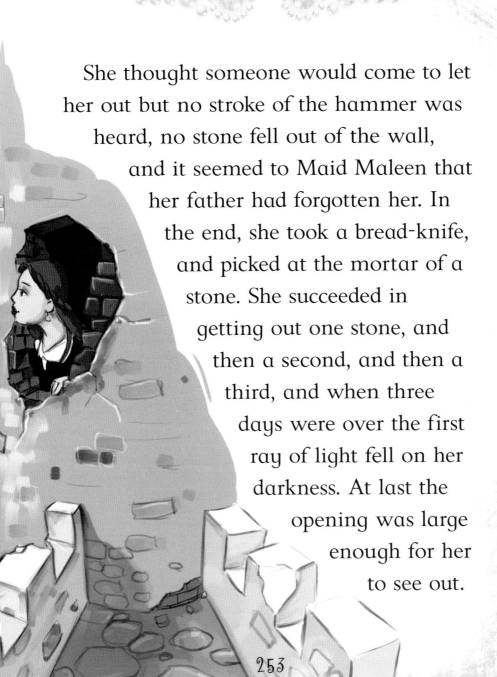

Maid Maleen

She thought someone would come to let
her out but no stroke of the hammer was
heard, no stone fell out of the wall,
and it seemed to Maid Maleen that
her father had forgotten her. In
the end, she took a bread-knife,
and picked at the mortar of a
stone. She succeeded in
getting out one stone, and
then a second, and then a
third, and when three
days were over the first
ray of light fell on her
darkness. At last the
opening was large
enough for her
to see out.

253

The sky was blue, and a fresh breeze blew, but her father's castle lay in ruins. The town and the villages were, so far as could be seen, destroyed by fire, and no human being was visible. An enemy had destroyed the whole kingdom and driven away the king and all the inhabitants.

Maid Maleen set out to find somewhere to live. After a long journey, she came to another country and went to the royal palace. At first she was ordered to go away, but at last the cook said that she might be a scullery maid.

The son of the king in whose kingdom she had arrived, was, however, the very man who had been betrothed to Maid Maleen. His father had chosen another bride for him, whose face was as ugly as her heart was wicked. The wedding was fixed, and the maiden had already arrived, but because of her great ugliness, she shut herself in her room, and allowed no one to see her. Maid Maleen had to take her meals from the kitchen. When the day came for the bride and the bridegroom to go to church, she was ashamed of her ugliness, and afraid that if she showed herself in the streets, she would be laughed at by the people.

So she said to Maid Maleen, "I have sprained my foot, and cannot walk well. Put on my wedding clothes and take my place, just for today!" Maid Maleen, however, refused. At last the bride said angrily, "If you do not obey me, I will order you to be killed at once."

Then Maid Maleen was forced to obey, and so she put on the bride's magnificent clothes and all her jewels. When she entered the hall, everyone was amazed at her great beauty. The bridegroom thought, 'She is just like my beautiful Maid Maleen, but she has long been shut up in the tower, and may have died.'

Maid Maleen

Then he took out a precious necklace, put it round her neck, and fastened the clasp. They travelled to the church, and the priest married them. The prince led her home, but she did not speak a single word the whole way.

When they got back to the royal palace, she hurried into the bride's chamber, took off the magnificent clothes and the jewels, dressed herself in her servant's clothes, but kept the jewel on her neck, which she had received from the bridegroom.

When the evening came, and the betrothed bride was led into the prince's apartment, she let her veil fall down over her face, so that he might not notice her ugly appearance.

The prince told her he liked her rich clothes and veil but said, "Where is the jewel that I gave you at the church door?"

"What jewel?" she answered, "You gave me no jewel."

"I myself put it around your neck. If you don't know that, then you are not the true bride." He drew the veil from her face, and sprang back, and said, "Who are you?"

"I am your betrothed bride, but because I feared the people would mock me when they saw me, I commanded the scullery-maid to dress herself in my clothes, and to go to church instead of me."

"Where is this girl?" said the prince. "Go and bring her here."

But instead of fetching the girl, she went out and told the servants that they must take the scullery maid into the courtyard and cut off her head. The servants took hold of Maid Maleen but she screamed so loudly for help, that the king's son heard her voice, and ordered them to set her free. Lights were brought, and then the prince saw on her neck the necklace that he had given her at the church door.

"You are the true bride, said he, "who

went with me to the church?"

She answered, "I am Maid Maleen, who for your sake was imprisoned for seven years in the darkness. Today, the sun is shining on me once more. I was married to you in the church, and I am your lawful wife."

Then they kissed each other, and were happy for the rest of their lives. The betrothed bride was banished from the kingdom as punishment for her lies.

Old Rinkrank

By the Brothers Grimm

ONCE UPON A TIME there was a king
who had a daughter. The king
had a glass mountain built, and
said that whoever could cross to the other
side of it without falling could marry his
daughter. There was a man who loved
the king's daughter very much, and he
asked the king if he could marry her.

"Yes," said the king, "if you can cross

the mountain without falling."

The princess had seen the prince and had fallen in love with him, so she said she would go over the mountain with him, and would hold him if he were about to fall. They set out together but when they were halfway up, the princess slipped and fell. The glass mountain opened, and shut her up inside it.

The prince could not see where she had gone, for the mountain closed up again immediately. The prince wept, and the king was miserable too. He had the mountain broken open where the princess had been lost. Although he would be able to get her out again, they could not find the place into which she had fallen.

Old Rinkrank

Meanwhile, the king's daughter had fallen deep down into a great cave. An old man with a very long grey beard was there. He told her that if she would do his housework she might live, but if not he would kill her.

263

The princess agreed. Each morning the old man took a ladder and set it up against the mountain and climbed to the top, and then he drew the ladder up after him. The princess had to cook his dinner, make his bed and do all his housework. When he came home again he always brought with him a heap of gold and silver, for he went out stealing all day.

When she had lived with him for some time, he called her 'Mother Mansrot', and she had to call him 'Old Rinkrank'. Once, when he was out, and she had made his bed and washed his dishes, she shut the doors and windows tight, though she left one little window open.

When Old Rinkrank came home, he

knocked at his door, and cried, "Mother Mansrot, open the door for me."

"No," said she, "Old Rinkrank, I will not open the door for you."

Then the old man said, "Here stand I, poor Rinkrank. Now wash my dishes, Mother Mansrot."

"I have washed your dishes already," said she. Then again he said, "Here stand I, poor Rinkrank. Now make my bed, Mother Mansrot."

"I have made your bed already," said she. Then again he said, "Here stand I, poor Rinkrank. Now open the door, Mother Mansrot."

"That I will not do," said she. Then he roared and beat on the door, but she stood fast and did not give in.

So he ran all around the house, and saw that the little window was open.

"I will look in and see what she is doing, and why she will not open the door for me," said Rinkrank. He tried to peep in, but could not get his head through because of his long beard. So he first put his beard through the open window, but just as he did so, the princess came by and pulled the window down with a cord that she had tied to it, and his beard was shut fast. He began to cry most piteously, for it hurt very much. He begged her to release him but she said not until he gave her the ladder with

which he climbed the mountain. Whether he wanted to or not, he had to tell her where the ladder was.

And so the princess took the ladder, fastened a very long ribbon to the window, and then set off up the mountain. When she reached the top she went to her father, and told him all that had happened. The king rejoiced greatly to have her back. Her prince was still there, so they followed the ribbon, found Old

Rinkrank inside the mountain, with all the gold and silver he had stolen.

Then the king had Old Rinkrank put in prison, and took all the treasure. The princess married her beloved, and lived happily in great magnificence and joy.

Ozma and the Little Wizard

By L Frank Baum

ONCE UPON A TIME there lived in the beautiful Emerald City, which lies in the centre of the fair Land of Oz, a lovely girl called Princess Ozma, who was ruler of that country. Among those who served her was a little, withered old man known as the Wizard of Oz.

This little wizard could do a good many things in magic, but he was a kind man, so, instead of fearing him because of his magic, everybody loved him.

Ozma decided one morning to make a journey to all parts of the country, so that she might discover if there was any wrong that ought to be righted. She asked the little wizard to accompany her and he was glad to go.

So the two left the Emerald City and wandered over the country for many days. Stopping one morning at a cottage, built beside the rocky path which led into a pretty valley beyond, Ozma asked a man, "Are you happy? Have you any complaint to make of your lot?"

And the man replied, "We are happy except for three mischievous imps that often come here to annoy us. If strangers pass through the valley the imps jeer at them, make horrid faces and often throw stones at them."

They told the good man that they would see what could be done to protect him from the imps and at once entered the valley.

Before long they came upon three caves, hollowed from the rocks, and in front of each cave squatted a queer little dwarf. They had big round ears, flat noses and wide grinning mouths, and dark hair came to points on top of their heads, much resembling horns. One of them suddenly reached out a hand and caught the dress of the princess, jerking it so that she nearly fell down, and another imp pushed the little wizard so hard that he bumped against Ozma and both unexpectedly sat down upon the ground.

At this the imps laughed boisterously and began running around in a circle, kicking dust upon the Royal Princess, who cried, "Wizard, do your duty!"

The wizard promptly obeyed. He opened his bag and muttered a spell.

Instantly the three Imps became three bushes — of a thorny stubby kind — with their roots in the ground.

"They can't help being good now, your

Highness," said the wizard.

But something must have been wrong with the wizard's magic, or the creatures had magic of their own, for no sooner were the words spoken than the bushes began to move. Pretty soon they began to slide over the ground, their roots dragging through the earth. One pricked the wizard so sharply with its thorns that he cried out in pain.

Ozma sprang behind a tree and shouted, "Quick! Wizard, transform them into something else."

The wizard heard. Grabbing from his bag the first magical tool he could find, he transformed the bushes into three pigs. That astonished the imps. In the shape of pigs – fat, roly-poly and cute – they scampered off a little distance and sat down to think.

Ozma drew a long breath and coming from behind the tree she said, "That is much better, for pigs must be quite harmless."

But the imps were now angry and had no intention of behaving. As Ozma and the little wizard turned, the three pigs rushed forwards, dashed between their legs, and tripped them up, so that both lost their balance and toppled over. As the wizard

274

tried to get up he was tripped again and fell across the back of the third pig, which carried him on a run until it dumped the little man in the river. Ozma could not help laughing at his woeful appearance.

The pigs tried to trip Ozma, too, but she ran around a stump and managed to keep out of their way. So the wizard scrambled out of the water again and mumbled a magic mutter to dry his clothes, then he hurried to help Ozma.

"This won't do," said the princess. "The pig imps would annoy travellers as much as the real imps. Transform them into something else, Wiz."

The wizard thought, then he changed

the pigs into three blue doves.

"Doves," said he, "are the most harmless things in the world."

But scarcely had he spoken when the doves flew at them and tried to peck out their eyes. When they shielded their eyes with their hands, two of the doves bit the wizard's fingers and another caught the pretty pink ear of the princess in its bill so that she cried out in pain.

"These birds are worse than pigs, Wizard," she called. "You must transform the imps into something that is not alive."

The wizard was pretty busy, just then, driving off the birds, but he managed to open his bag of magic and find a charm, which changed the doves into three buttons. As they fell to the ground he picked them up and smiled. The wizard placed the buttons in a little box, which he put in his jacket pocket.

"Now," said he, "the imps cannot annoy travellers. We shall take them with us to the Emerald City."

"But we dare not use the buttons," said Ozma, smiling once more now that the danger was over.

"Why not?" asked the wizard. "I intend to sew them upon my coat and watch them carefully. The spirits of the imps are still in the buttons, and after a time they will be sorry for their naughtiness and may decide to be very good in the future. When they feel that way, I shall then restore them to their proper forms."

"Ah, that is magic well worthwhile," exclaimed Ozma, well pleased. "There is no doubt, my friend, but that you are a very clever wizard.

The Twelve Huntsmen

By the Brothers Grimm

ONCE UPON A TIME there was a prince who was engaged to a princess whom he dearly loved. One day as he sat by her side feeling very happy, he received news that his father was lying at the point of death, and wanted to see him before his end. So he said to his love, "Alas! I must go off and leave you, but take this ring and wear it as a remembrance of me, and when I am king I will return and fetch you home."

Then he rode off, and when he reached his father he found him very near death.

The sick king said, "Dearest son, I have wanted to see you again before my end. Promise me, I beg of you, that you will marry who I choose," and he then named the daughter of a nearby king. The prince was so sad that he could think of nothing but his father, and cried, "Yes, yes, dear father, whatever you desire shall be done." And then the king closed his eyes and died.

After the prince had been proclaimed king, he felt that he must keep the promise he had made to his father, so he sent to ask for the hand of the king's daughter, which was granted to him.

Now, his first love heard of this, and the thought of her lover's desertion made her so sad that she pined away and nearly died. Her father said to her, "My dearest child, why are you so unhappy? If there is anything you wish for, say so, and you shall have it."

His daughter thought for a moment, and then said, "Dear father, I wish for eleven girls as near as possible to my height, age and appearance."

So the king had his kingdom searched till eleven maidens of the same height, age and appearance as his daughter were found and brought to the palace.

Then the princess asked for twelve

complete huntsmen's suits to be made, all exactly alike, and the eleven maidens had to dress themselves in eleven of the suits, while she herself put on the twelfth. After this she said goodbye to her father, and rode off with her girls to the court of her former love.

Here she enquired whether the king wanted some huntsmen, and if he would not take them all as his servants. The king saw her but did not recognize her, and said he would gladly hire them all. So they became the royal huntsmen.

Now, the king had a most remarkable lion, for it knew every hidden secret. One evening the lion said to the king, "You think you have got twelve huntsmen?"

"Yes, certainly," said the king.

"There you are mistaken," said the lion, "they are twelve maidens."

"That cannot possibly be," replied the king, "how do you mean to prove that?"

"Just have a number of dried peas scattered over the floor of your antechamber," said the lion, "and you will soon see. Men have a strong, firm tread, so that if they happen to walk over peas not one will stir, but girls trip and slip and slide, so that the peas roll all about."

Fortunately one of the king's servants had become very fond of the young huntsmen, and he went to them and said, "The lion wants to persuade the king that you are only girls," and he told them all the plot.

The princess thanked him, and after he was gone she said to her maidens, "Make every effort to tread firmly on the peas."

Next morning, when the king sent for

his twelve huntsmen, and they passed through the anteroom — which was plentifully strewn with peas — they trod so firmly and walked with such a steady, strong step that not one pea moved. After they were gone the king said to the lion, "There now — you have been telling lies — you see they walk like men."

"Because they knew they were being put to the test," answered the lion, "and so they made an effort. Just have a dozen spinning-wheels placed in the anteroom. When they pass through you'll see how pleased and interested they will be, quite unlike any man."

But the good-natured servant went to the huntsmen and told them this fresh plot. Then, as soon as the princess was alone with her maidens, she exclaimed, "Now, make sure you don't even look at those spinning-wheels."

When the king sent for his twelve huntsmen next morning they walked through the anteroom without even casting a glance at the spinning-wheels.

The king said once more to the lion, "You have deceived me again — they are men, for they never once looked at the spinning-wheels."

So the twelve huntsmen continued to follow the king, and he grew daily fonder of them. One day whilst they were all out hunting the news was brought that the king's intended bride was on her way.

When the true bride heard of this she
felt as though a knife had pierced her
heart, and she fell fainting to the ground.
The king ran up to help, and began
drawing off his gloves. Then he saw the
ring that he had given to his first love,
and as he gazed into her face he knew
her again. His heart
was so touched that
he kissed her, and
as she opened

her eyes, he cried, "I am yours and you are mine, and no power on earth can alter that."

To the other princess he sent a messenger to beg her to return to her own kingdom. "For," said he, "I have a wife, and he who finds an old key again does not need a new one."

And so the wedding was celebrated with great joy, and the lion was the chief guest, for after all he had told the truth.

The Crow

By Andrew Lang

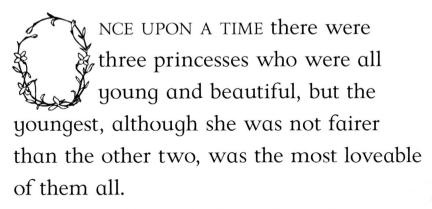

NCE UPON A TIME there were three princesses who were all young and beautiful, but the youngest, although she was not fairer than the other two, was the most loveable of them all.

About half a mile from the palace in which they lived there stood a castle. It was almost a ruin, but the garden that surrounded it was a mass of blooming flowers, and in this garden the youngest princess often used to walk.

One day when she was pacing to and fro under the lime trees, a black crow hopped out of a rose bush in front of her. The poor beast was all torn and bleeding, and the kind little princess was quite unhappy about it.

When the crow saw this it turned to her and said, "I am not really a black crow, but an enchanted prince, who has been doomed to spend his youth in misery. If you liked, princess, you could save me. But you would have to say goodbye to all your own people and come and be my constant companion in a ruined castle. There is only one room in it fit to live in, in which there is a golden bed. There you will have to live all by yourself, and don't forget that whatever you may see or hear in the night you must not scream out, for if you give as much as a single cry my sufferings will be doubled."

The good-natured princess felt so sorry for the black crow that she left her home and her family at once, and hurried to the ruined castle to take possession of the room with the golden bed.

When night approached she lay down, but though she shut her eyes tight, sleep would not come. At midnight she heard to her great horror someone coming

along the passage, and in a minute her
door was flung wide open and a troop of
strange beings entered the
room, goblins, sprites,
imps, witches and
trolls. They lit a
fire then

placed a great cauldron of boiling water on it. When they had done this, they approached the bed on which the trembling girl lay, and, screaming and yelling all the time, they dragged her towards the cauldron. She nearly died with fright, but she never uttered a sound. Then suddenly the cock crew, and all the evil spirits vanished. At the same moment the crow appeared and hopped all round the room with joy. It thanked the princess, and said that it already felt a bit better.

So she lived in solitude all day, and at night she would have been frightened, had she not been so brave. Every day the crow thanked her for her bravery, and assured her that its sufferings were far less than they had been the day before.

And so two years passed this way, when one day the crow came to the princess and said, "In another year I shall be freed from the spell I am under at present, because then the seven years will be over. But before I can go back to my natural form, you must go out into the world and take a job as a maidservant."

The young princess agreed at once, and for a whole year she served as a maid. In

spite of her youth and beauty she was
very badly treated, and suffered many
things. One evening, when she was sitting
at her spinning-wheel, and had worked
her little white hands weary, she heard a
rustling beside her and a cry of joy. Then
she saw a handsome youth standing
beside her. He knelt down at her feet and
kissed her weary white hands.

"I am the prince," he said, "who you in
your goodness, when I was wandering
about in the shape of a black crow, freed
from the most awful torments. Come
now to my castle with me as my bride,
and let us live there happily together."

So they went to the castle where they
had both suffered so much. But when

they reached it, it was difficult to believe
that it was the same, for it had all been
rebuilt and filled with beautiful furniture,
rich carpets and cheerful servants and
friends. And there they lived for a
hundred years, a hundred years of joy
and happiness.

The Twelve Brothers

A German fairy tale

ONCE UPON A TIME a king and a queen lived happily together, and they had twelve children, all of whom were boys. One day the king said to his wife, "If our thirteenth child is a girl, all her twelve brothers must die, so that she may be very rich and the kingdom hers alone."

The queen grieved over the sad fate of her sons and refused to be comforted.

In the end she warned her sons and urged them to run for their lives. She blessed them and they set out into the wood.

And in the middle of it, where it was thickest and darkest, they came upon a enchanted house, which stood empty.

"Here," they said, "we will live, and you, Benjamin, you are the youngest and weakest, you shall stay at home and keep house for us. We others will go out to look for food." So they lived for ten years in this little house, and the time slipped merrily away.

In the meantime their little sister at home was growing up quickly. She was kind-hearted, and she had a gold star right in the middle of her forehead. One washing day at the palace the girl saw twelve shirts hanging up to dry, and so she asked her mother, "Who in the world do these shirts belong to? Surely they are far too small for my father?" And the queen answered sadly, "Dear child, they belong to your twelve brothers." "But where are my twelve brothers?" said the girl. "I have never heard of them."

Then the queen had to tell her all that had happened, and when she had finished her daughter said, "Do not cry, dearest mother, I will go and seek my brothers.

So she went straight into the middle of the big wood. She walked all day, and in the evening came to the little enchanted house. She stepped in and found a youth who, marvelling at her beauty, at the royal robes she wore, and at the golden star on her forehead, asked her where she came from and where she was going.

"I am a princess," she answered, "and am seeking my twelve brothers."

Then Benjamin saw that it must be his younger sister, and said, "I am Benjamin, your brother."

So they wept for joy, and kissed and hugged each other again and again.

And when the brothers came home Benjamin said, "Our sister is here!" and the princess stepped forward looking so lovely and sweet and charming that they all fell in love with her on the spot.

They arranged that she should stay at home with Benjamin and help him in the house, while the rest of the brothers went out hunting. And Benjamin and his sister cooked their meals for them. Besides this, she kept the house in order, tidied all the rooms, and made herself generally useful — and they all lived happily together.

There was a little garden around the enchanted house, in which grew twelve

tall white flowers. One day the girl,
plucked the twelve flowers, meaning to

give one to each of her brothers. But as
soon as she plucked them, her brothers
turned into twelve ravens. They flew
croaking over the wood, and the house

and garden vanished too. The poor girl found herself all alone, and as she looked around she noticed an old woman standing close beside her, who said, "My child, what have you done? Why didn't you leave the flowers alone? They were your twelve brothers. Now they are changed forever into ravens."

The girl asked, sobbing, "Is there no means of setting them free?"

"No," said the old woman, "there is only one way in the whole world, and it is so difficult, for you would have to be silent and not laugh for seven years, and if you spoke a single word, your silence would all have been in vain, and that one word would kill your brothers."

Then the girl said to herself, "If that is
all I am quite sure I can free my
brothers." So she searched for a high tree,
and when she had found one, she climbed
it and sat spinning all day long, never
laughing or speaking one word.

Now it happened one day that a king
who was hunting looked up and beheld
the beautiful princess with the golden star
on her forehead. He was so enchanted by
her beauty that he asked her on the spot
to be his wife. She gave no answer, but
nodded slightly with her head. Then he
climbed up the tree himself, lifted her
down, put her on his horse and bore her
home to his wonderful palace.

The marriage was celebrated with

much ceremony, but the bride neither spoke nor laughed.

When they had lived happily together for a few years, the king's mother, who was a wicked woman, began to accuse the young queen of so many bad things, that at last the king let himself be talked round, and condemned his wife to death.

So a great fire was lit in the courtyard of the palace, where she was to be burnt, and the king watched the proceedings from an upper window, crying bitterly. But just as she had been bound to the stake, and the flames were licking her garments, the very last moment of the seven years had come. Then a sudden rushing sound was heard in the air, and twelve ravens were seen flying overhead. They swooped downwards, and as soon as they touched the ground they turned into her twelve brothers.

They put out the fire, and, unbinding their dear sister from the stake, they kissed and hugged her again and again. And now that she was able to open her mouth and speak, she told the king why she had been dumb and not able to laugh.

The king rejoiced greatly and they all lived happily ever afterwards.

The Secret Princess

A traditional Russian fairy tale

ONCE UPON A TIME there was a prince and princess who lived happily together. They were very fond of each other and had nothing to worry them, but at last the prince grew restless. He longed to go out into the world to try his strength in battle against some enemy and win all kinds of honour.

So he called his army together and gave orders to start for a distant country where there ruled a cruel prince who ill-treated his subjects. The prince said goodbye to his wife, and set off with his army across the seas.

I cannot say whether the voyage was short or long, but at last he reached the country and marched on, defeating all who came in his way. But this did not last long, for in time he came to a mountain pass, where a large army was waiting to take the prince himself prisoner.

He was carried off to prison and now our poor friend had a very bad time indeed. All night long the prisoners were chained up, and in the morning they were yoked together like oxen and had to plough the land till it grew dark.

This state of things went on for three years before the prince found any means of sending news of himself to his dear princess, but at last he managed to send this letter:

> Sell all our castles and palaces, and then come and deliver me out of this horrible prison.

The princess received the letter, read it, and wept bitterly as she said to herself, "How can I rescue my dearest husband?"

She thought, and at last an idea came to her. She cut off all her beautiful long brown hair and dressed herself in boy's clothes. Then she took her lute and went forth into the wide world.

The princess travelled through many
lands before she got to the town where
the bad prince lived. When she got there
she walked all round the palace and at
the back she saw the prison.
Then she went into the great court
in front of the palace,
and taking her
lute in her
hand, began to
play and sing as
beautifully as she
could. When the
heathen prince
heard this
touching song,
sung by such a

lovely voice, he had the singer brought before him.

"Welcome, O lute player," said he. "Where do you come from?"

"My country, sire, is far away across many seas," said the princess, "For years I have been wandering about the world and gaining my living by my music."

The heathen prince replied, "Stay here a few days, and when you wish to leave I will give you what you ask for in your song – your heart's desire."

So the lute player stayed on in the palace and sang and played almost all day long to the prince.

After three days the lute player came to say goodbye to the prince.

"Well," said the prince, "what do you want as your reward?"

"Sire, give me one of your prisoners," she replied, "You have so many in your prison, and I should be glad of a companion on my journeys. When I hear his happy voice as I travel along I shall think of you."

"Come along then," said the prince, "choose who you want." And he took the lute player through the prison himself.

The princess picked out her husband and although the heathen prince was not happy with her choice, she took him with her on her journey. Their journey lasted a great many days, but he never found out who she was, although he asked many times. Instead, the secret princess led him nearer to his own country.

When they reached the frontier the prisoner said, "Let me go now, kind lad. I am no common prisoner, but the prince of this country. Let me go free and ask what you will as your reward."

"Do not speak of reward now," said the lute player. "Go in peace." And so they parted ways. The princess took a short way home, got there before the prince and changed her dress. An hour later all the people in the palace were running to and fro and crying out with great excitement, "Our prince has come back! Our prince has returned to us!"

The prince greeted everyone kindly, but

he would not so much as look at the princess. Then he called all his council and ministers together and said to them, "See what sort of a wife I have. She is happy to see me, but when I was pining in prison, she did nothing to help me."

And his council answered, "Sire, when news was brought from you the princess disappeared and no one knew where she went. She only returned today."

Then the prince was very angry and cried, "You would never have seen me again, if a young lute player had not rescued me. I shall remember him with love and gratitude as long as I live."

Whilst the prince was sitting with his council, the princess put on her travelling cloak to disguise herself again. She took her lute, and slipping into the court sang, clear and sweet. As soon as the prince heard this song he ran out to meet the lute player, took him by the hand and led him into the palace.

"Here," he cried, "is the boy who released me from my prison. And now, my true friend, ask for anything and I will give you your heart's desire."

"Sir, I ask of you what I asked and got from the bad prince. But this time I don't mean to give up what I get. I want you!" And as she spoke she threw off her cloak and everyone saw it was the princess.

Who can tell how happy the prince was? He held a great feast for his whole

kingdom, and everyone came and rejoiced with him for a week.

I was there too, and ate and drank many good things. I shall not forget it as long as I live.

From Rags to Riches

The Dirty Shepherdess

By Paul Sébillot

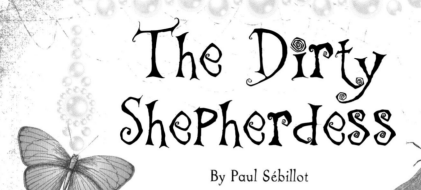

O NCE UPON A TIME there lived a king who had two daughters, and he loved them both with all his heart. When they grew up, he made up his mind that he would give his kingdom to the one who could best show how much she loved him.

So he called the eldest princess and said to her, "How much do you love me?"

"You are the apple of my eye," she said.

"Ah!" exclaimed the king, "you are indeed a good daughter."

Then he sent for the younger daughter, and asked her how much she loved him.

"I love you, my father," she answered, "as I love the salt in my food."

This made the king very angry for salt seemed a very little thing to him, and he ordered her to leave the court, and never appear before him again. The poor princess made a bundle of her jewels and her best dresses and hurriedly left the castle where she was born.

She walked away, without knowing what was to become of her, for she had never been shown how to work. And as she was afraid that no one would want

to hire a girl with such a pretty
face, she decided to make
herself as ugly as she could.

She took off her royal
dress and put on some
horrible old rags belonging
to a beggar. After that she
smeared mud all over her hands
and face, and shook her hair into a
great tangle. After walking for a great
many days she came to a neighbouring
kingdom. She arrived at a large farm
where they needed a shepherdess, and
were glad to hire her.

One day when she was watching her
sheep in a lonely part of the country, she
felt a wish to dress herself in her robes of

splendour. She washed herself in the stream and put on her fine robes, which she always carried with her. The king's son, who had lost his way out hunting, saw her from a distance, and wished to look at her closer. But the girl ran into the wood as swiftly as a bird.

When she was quite safe, she put on her rags again, and smeared mud over her face and hands. However the young prince, who was both hot and thirsty, found his way to the farm to ask for a drink, and he asked the name of the beautiful lady that kept the sheep. At this everyone began to laugh, for they said that the shepherdess was one of the ugliest and dirtiest creatures under the sun.

The prince thought some witchcraft must be at work, and he went away before the return of the shepherdess.

But the prince thought often of the lovely maiden. At last he dreamed of nothing else, and grew thinner day by day until his parents promised to do all they could to make him as happy as he once was. He dared not tell them the truth, so he only said that he should like some bread baked by the shepherdess from the distant farm.

The maiden showed no surprise at receiving such an order, but merely asked for some flour, salt and water. Before beginning her work she washed herself carefully, and even put on her rings. While she was baking, one of her rings slid into the dough. When she had finished she dirtied herself again so that she became as ugly as before.

The loaf was brought to the king's son, who ate it with pleasure. But in it he found the ring of the princess, and declared to his parents that he would marry the girl whom that ring fitted.

So the king made a proclamation through his whole kingdom and ladies

came from afar to win the prince. But the
ring was so tiny that even those who had
the smallest hands could only get it on
their little fingers. In a short
time all the maidens
of the kingdom,
including the
peasant girls,
had tried on
the ring, and
the king was
just about to
announce that
their efforts had
been in vain, when
the prince said he had
not yet seen the shepherdess.

They sent for her, and she arrived covered with rags, but with her hands cleaner than usual, so that she could easily slip on the ring. The king's son declared that this was the girl he would marry. When his parents remarked that the girl was only a keeper of sheep the maiden said that she was born a princess, and that, if they would give her some water and leave her alone in a room for a few minutes, she would show them.

They did what she asked, and when she entered in a magnificent dress, she looked so beautiful that all believed her. The king's son asked if she would marry him. The princess then told her story, and asked to invite her father to the wedding.

It was with great joy that the princess's father heard that she was alive and that a king's son asked her hand in marriage, for he had been deeply sorry for his hard words to her, and he hurried to be present at the ceremony.

By the orders of the bride, at the wedding feast they served her father bread without salt, and meat without seasoning. Seeing him make faces, and eat very little, his daughter asked if he liked his food.

"No," he replied, "the dishes are carefully cooked, but they are all so dreadfully tasteless."

"Did I not tell you, my father, that salt was the best thing in life?"

The king hugged his daughter, and begged her forgiveness. Then, for the rest of the wedding feast they gave him bread made with salt, and dishes with seasoning, and he said they were the very best he had ever eaten.

The Mother and the Daughter who Worshipped the Sun

By Flora Annie Steel

NCE UPON A TIME there lived a mother and a daughter who worshipped the Sun. Though they were very poor, they never forgot to honour the Sun, giving everything they earned to it except two small cornmeal cakes — one of which the mother ate, while the other was the daughter's share. Every day one cake apiece, that was all.

Now it so happened that one day, when the mother was out at work, the daughter grew hungry, and ate her cake before dinnertime. Just as she had finished it a priest came by, and begged for some bread. So the daughter broke off half of her mother's piece and gave it to the priest in the name of the Sun.

By and by the mother returned, very hungry for her dinner, and lo and behold there was only half a cake left.

"Where is the remainder of the bread?" she asked.

"I ate my share of the cake," said the

daughter, "and just as I finished, a priest came begging, so I was obliged to give him your half."

"A fine story!" said the mother, in a rage. "I believe you gave my cake in order to save yours!"

The daughter protested that she really had finished her cake before the priest came begging. She promised to give her mother her share the next day. But her mother told her to leave home, saying, "I will have no greedyguts in my house!"

So the daughter wandered away into the wilds, crying. When she had gone a long, long way, she became very

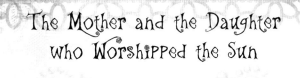

tired and climbed into a pipal tree for safety. She still cried while she rested among the branches.

After a time, a young prince came to the tree and lay down to sleep. As he lay there, he looked so beautiful. The daughter could not keep her eyes off him, and so her tears flowed down onto him like a summer shower upon the young man's face. He woke with a start.

Thinking it was raining, he rose to look at the sky, and see where this sudden storm had come from, but far and near not a cloud was to be seen. So he swung himself into the tree, and lo and behold, he found a beautiful maiden sitting in the tree, weeping sadly.

"Where do you come from, fair stranger?" said he, and with tears in her eyes she told him she was homeless and motherless. He fell in love with her sweet face and soft words, so he asked her to be his bride, and she went with him to the palace, her heart full of gratitude to the Sun, who had sent her such good luck.

Everything she could desire was hers, but when the other women talked of their homes she held her tongue, for she was ashamed of hers.

Everyone thought she must be some great princess, she was so lovely and magnificent, but in her heart of hearts she knew she was nothing of the kind, so every day she prayed to the Sun that her mother might not find her out.

But one day, when she was sitting alone in her beautiful palace, her mother appeared, ragged and poor as ever. She had heard of her daughter's good fortune, and had come to share it.

"And you shall share it," pleaded her daughter. "I will give you back far more than I ever took from you, if only you will not disgrace me before my prince."

"Ungrateful creature!" stormed the mother, "did you forget that it was through my act that your good fortune came to you? If I had not sent you out into the world, where would you have found so fine a husband?"

"I might have starved!" wept the daughter, "and now you come to destroy me again. Oh great Sun, help me now!"

Just then the prince came to the door, and the poor daughter was ready to die of shame and vexation, but when she turned to where her mother had sat, there was nothing to be seen but a golden stool, the like of which had never been seen on earth before.

"My princess," asked the prince,

astonished, "where does that golden stool come from?"

"From my mother's house," replied the daughter, full of gratitude to the great Sun, who had saved her from disgrace.

"If there are such wonderful things to be seen in your mother's house," said the prince, "I must go and see it. Tomorrow we will set out on our journey, and you shall show me all it contains."

In vain the daughter put forward one excuse after another. The prince's curiosity had been aroused by the sight of the marvellous golden stool, and he was not to be put off.

Then the daughter cried once more to the Sun, in her distress, saying, "Oh gracious Sun, help me now!"

But no answer came, and with a heavy heart she set out the next day to show the prince her mother's house. A fine procession they made, with horsemen and footmen clothed in royal liveries surrounding the coach, where the daughter sat, her heart sinking at every step.

And when they came close to where her mother's hut used to stand, there on the horizon was a shining, flaming golden palace that glittered and shone like solid sunshine. Within and without all was gold. A golden mother came out to greet them. She spoke graciously, for she remembered

nothing about her trip to the prince's palace!

There they stayed, admiring the countless marvels of the Sun palace for three days, and when the third day was over, the prince, more in love with his bride than ever, turned homewards. But when he came to the spot where he had first seen the glittering golden palace from afar, he thought he would take just one more look at the wondrous sight, and lo, there was nothing to be seen except a low thatched hovel!

He turned to his bride, full of anger, and said, "You are a witch, and have tricked me! Confess, if you would not have me strike you dead!"

But the daughter fell on her knees, saying, "My gracious prince, believe me, I have done nothing! I am a poor homeless girl. I prayed to the Sun, and the Sun helped me!"

Then she told the whole story from beginning to end, and the prince was so well pleased that from that day he too worshipped the Sun.

The Princess and the Lion

A traditional Spanish fairy tale

HERE WAS ONCE A POOR GIRL who worked as a cowherd. One morning she was driving her cows through the meadows when she heard a loud groan. She rushed to the spot and found the noise came from a lion, which lay stretched upon the ground.

You can guess how frightened she was! But the lion seemed in so much pain that she drew nearer until she saw he had a

From Rags to Riches

342

large thorn in one foot. She pulled out the thorn, bound up the paw, and the lion was very grateful. He licked her hand with his big rough tongue.

When the girl had finished, she went back to find the cows, but they had gone, and though she hunted everywhere she could not find them. Her master scolded her bitterly for losing the cows.

After that she had to take the donkeys to the woods to feed, until one morning, she heard a groan, which sounded quite human. She went straight to the source of the noise, and saw the same lion lying with a deep wound across his face.

This time she was not afraid at all, and ran towards him, washing the wound and laying soothing herbs upon it. When she had bound it up the lion thanked her in the same manner as before.

After that she returned to her herd of donkeys, but they were nowhere to be seen. She searched but they had vanished!

Then she had to go home and confess to her master, who scolded her severely. "Now go," he said, "and see to the pigs!"

So the next day she took the pigs out, and found them such good feeding grounds that they grew fatter every day.

A year passed by, and one morning when the maiden was out with her pigs she heard a groan. She ran to see what it was, and found her old friend the lion, wounded, lying under a tree.

She washed his wounds one by one,
and laid healing herbs upon them. And
the lion licked her hands. After he had
gone she ran to the place where she
had left her pigs, but they had vanished.

The maiden looked everywhere and at
last she thought that if she climbed a tree
she might see them. But as soon as she
was up the tree, something happened that
quite put the pigs out of her head. A
handsome young man was coming down
the path, and when he had almost
reached the tree he pulled aside a rock
and disappeared behind it.

The maiden rubbed her eyes and
waited, and at dawn the next morning
the rock moved to one side and a lion

came out. The maiden thought to herself, 'I will not move from here until I discover who that young man is.'

That evening the young man came back, so she came down from the tree and begged him to tell her his name.

The young man looked very pleased to see her, and said that he was a prince enchanted by a powerful giant, and all day he was forced to appear as the lion whom she had so often helped. More than this, it was the giant who had stolen her animals in revenge for her kindness.

So the girl asked him, "What can I do to disenchant you?"

He said it was difficult, because the only way was to get a lock of hair from the head of a princess, to spin it, and to make it a cloak from for the giant.

"Very well," answered the girl, "I will go to the city, and knock at the door of the king's palace, and ask the princess to take me as a servant." She went straight to the palace to ask for work.

"You will have to do kitchen work," she was told, and she agreed.

Every day the maiden arranged her hair, and made herself look very neat and smart, and everyone admired and praised her, until the princess heard of it. She sent for the girl, and when she saw how nicely she had dressed her hair, the princess told her she was to come and comb hers.

Now the hair of the princess was very

thick and long, and shone like the sun.
The girl combed it until it was brighter
than ever. The princess was pleased, and
told her to come every day until at length
the girl took courage, and begged
permission to cut off one lock.

The princess, who was very proud of
her hair, did not like the idea of parting
with any of it, but she said, "You may
have it, then, on condition that you shall
find me a handsome prince to marry!"

And the girl answered that she would
try. She cut off the lock, and wove it into
a coat that glittered like silk, and brought
it to the young man. He told her to carry
it straight to the giant.

So the maiden climbed up the

mountain, but before she reached the top the giant heard her, and rushed out breathing fire and flame. She called out loudly that she had brought him the coat, and he grew quiet.

The giant tried on the coat, and seemed quite pleased, and so he asked her what he could give her in return. The maiden said that the only reward the giant could give her was to take the spell off the lion, so that he could return to his human form.

The giant would not hear of it at first, but in the end he gave in, and told her how it must be done. She had to kill the lion, burn him, then cast his ashes into a stream. The prince would come out of the water, free from the enchantment.

Weeping, she came down the mountain and joined the prince. When he heard her story he comforted her, and told her to do what the giant had said.

So in the morning when the prince took on his lion's form, she took a knife and killed him. She then burnt him, cast his ashes into the water, and out of the water came the prince, beautiful as the day.

Then the young man thanked the

maiden for all she had done for him, and
asked if she would marry him. But the
maiden answered sadly that she had
promised the princess when she cut off
her hair that the prince would marry her.

But the prince replied, "If it is the
princess I think it is, we must go quickly.
Come with me."

So they went together to the king's
palace. And when the king and queen
and princess saw the young man, a great
joy filled their hearts, for he was their
eldest son, and the princess's brother, who
had been enchanted and lost to them.

So he told them he was to marry the
girl who had saved him, and a great feast
was made. The maiden became a

princess, and she richly deserved all the honours showered upon her. Afterwards she invited the mighty prince of a neighbouring country to come and marry the princess, and they all lived happily ever after.

The Red Slippers

By Gertrude Landa

ROSY-RED WAS A SWEET LITTLE GIRL, with beautiful blue eyes, soft pink cheeks and glorious red hair. Her mother died the day she was born, but her grandmother looked after her. She was very happy. All day long she sang, and so lovely was her voice that birds gathered on the trees to listen to her.

On her first birthday, her father's gift to her was a pair of red leather slippers.

Now, although neither she nor her father knew it, they were magic slippers, which grew larger as her feet grew.

Rosy-red was only a child and so did not know that slippers don't usually grow.

One day, Rosy-red returned from the woods to find her grandmother gone and three strange women in the house. "Who are you?" she asked.

"I am your new mother," answered the eldest of the three, "and these are my daughters, your two new sisters."

Her father appeared then and spoke

kindly, telling her he had married again, because he was lonely and that her stepmother and stepsisters would be good to her. But Rosy-red hastened away to her own little room and hid her slippers of which she was very proud.

"If they have turned my dear granny out of doors, they will take my beautiful slippers from me," she sobbed.

After that, Rosy-red sang no more. She was made to collect firewood for the fire and draw water from the well. She struggled with the heavy bucket, the weight of which made her arms and her back ache with pain. Sometimes her cruel and selfish stepsisters beat her. Often they went out to parties and she had to act as their maid. Rosy-red did not mind, she was only happy when they were out of the house. Only then did she sing softly to herself, and the birds came to listen.

So the years passed away and Rosy-red grew into a beautiful young woman. Once, when her father was away from home, her stepsisters went to a wedding dance. They told her not to forget to draw water from the well, and warned her that if she forgot they would beat her when they returned.

So Rosy-red went out in the darkness to draw water. She lowered the bucket, but the cord broke and the pail fell to the bottom of the well. She ran back home for a long stick with a hook at the end,

and as she put it into the water she sang,
"Swing and sweep until all does cling,
and to the surface safely bring."
It so happened that a sleeping genie
dwelt at the bottom of the well.
He could only be awakened
by a spell, and although
Rosy-red did not
know it, these
words were the spell.
The genie awoke,
and he was so pleased
with the sweet voice
that he fastened the
bucket to the stick and
put some beautiful
jewels inside.

"Oh, how beautiful," cried Rosy-red when she saw the glittering gems. "I will give these jewels to my sisters. Perhaps then they will be kinder to me."

She waited until the sisters returned from the dance and showed them the jewels. For a moment they were too dazed to speak when they saw the sparkling precious stones. Then they asked how she came by them. Rosy-red told them of the words she had sung.

"Ah, we thought so," said the sisters, to her horror. "The jewels are ours. We hid them in the well for safety."

They told her to hurry off to bed, then snatching the bucket they hurried off to the well. They lowered the bucket and sang the words. At least they thought they sang, but their voices were harsh. The sleeping genie awoke again, but he did not like their croaking voices.

"I will teach you to disturb my sleep with hideous noises," he said. "Here are some more croakers," and he filled the bucket with slimy toads and frogs.

The sisters were so angry that they ran back home and dragged Rosy-red from her bed. "You cheat," they exclaimed. "Off you go. You cannot remain in this house another day."

Rosy-red had only time to snatch her pretty red slippers and put them on. On and on she walked, much further into the woods than ever before. The magic slippers guided her, and as darkness fell she noticed a light a short distance away.

When she got quite close, Rosy-red saw that the light came from a cave. An old woman came out to meet her. It was her grandmother, but Rosy-red did not recognize her. Granny, however, at once knew her. "Come in, my child, and take shelter from the rain," she said kindly.

The inside of the cave was quite cosy, and Rosy-red, who was completely exhausted, quickly fell fast asleep. A few hours later, she awoke with a start.

"Where are my red slippers," she cried.

She put her hand in the pocket of her tattered dress, but could only find one.

"I must have lost the other," she sobbed.

"I must go out and look for it."

"No, no," said Granny. "You cannot do that. A storm is raging."

Rosy-red sobbed herself to sleep, but was woken up again by voices. She crept into a corner of the cave and listened.

A man was speaking. "Do you know who this red slipper belongs to?" he was asking. "I found it in the woods."

Rosy-red was moving forwards when she heard her granny say, "No, no, I don't know." The man left.

Granny came back into the cave and said, "I'm sorry, but he might be a messenger from your sisters, and I cannot let anyone take you back to them."

The next day, the man called again,

this time with several servants. Again, Rosy-red concealed herself.

"I am a prince," said the man, "and I must meet the wearer of this shoe. Only a graceful and beautiful girl can wear such a dainty slipper." Day after day he came, each time with more servants. Finally, he came with one hundred and one servants.

"The girl I seek is here," he said. "Deny it no longer. My servants heard a young girl singing here yesterday."

Rosy-red stepped out bravely, wearing her one red slipper. The stranger, bowing before her, held out the other slipper, and placed it on her foot. It fitted her perfectly.

"Many girls have tried to put

on that shoe," said the young man, "but all have failed. Let us get to know each other, and if you like me I have sworn to make you my bride. I am a king's son, and you shall be a princess."

So Rosy-red left the cave with her granny, and was led through the woods to her new home where she knew only happiness. And she always wore her magic red slippers.

The Old Woman in the Wood

By the Brothers Grimm

A POOR SERVANT GIRL was once travelling through a great forest, when she got lost. She began to weep bitterly and said, "What can a poor girl like me do now? I do not know how to get out of the forest, no human being lives in it, so I will certainly starve."

She walked about and looked for a

road, but could find none. When it was evening she seated herself under a tree, gave herself into God's keeping, and decided to wait and see what happened.

When she had sat there for a while, a white dove came flying to her with a little golden key in its beak. It put the little key in her hand, and said, "Do you see that great tree? In it is a little lock. It opens with this tiny key, and there you will find food enough, and suffer no more hunger."

So she went to the tree and opened it, and found milk in a

little dish. There was white bread to break into it, so that she could eat her fill. When she was satisfied, she said, "It is now the time when the hens at home go to roost. I am so tired, I wish I could go to bed too."

And the dove flew to her again, and brought another golden key in its bill, and said, "Open that tree there and you will find a bed." So she opened it, and found a beautiful white bed, with the softest pillows and sheets of clean linen. She prayed to God to protect her during the night, and lay down and slept.

In the morning the dove came for the third time, and again brought a little key and said, "Open that tree there, and you will find clothes." And when the girl opened it, she found a dress of soft green silk embroidered with gold and silver threads hung with tiny crystals and diamonds. With it were tiny gold slippers, more splendid than those of any princess.

So she lived there for some time, and the dove came every day and provided her with all she needed, and it was a quiet, good life.

Once, however, the dove came and said, "Will you do something for me?"

"With all my heart," said the girl.

Then the little dove said, "I will guide you to a small house. Enter it, and there you will see an old woman sitting by the fire. She will say 'Good day', but give her no answer, let her do what she will and pass by her. Further on, there is a door. Open it, and you will enter into a room where rings of all kinds are lying. Leave the ones with jewels where they are, and look for a plain one, and bring it here to me as quickly as you can."

The girl went to the little house, and went inside. There sat an old woman who stared when she saw her, and said, "Good day my child." The girl gave her no answer, and passing by her, opened a door.

"What are you doing?" cried the old woman. She seized her by the gown, saying, "This is my house — no one can go in there." But the girl stayed silent and went straight into the room. There on the table lay a number of rings, which gleamed and glittered before her eyes. She turned them over and looked for the plain one, but could not find it.

While she was searching, she saw the old woman sneaking away with a bird cage in her hand. So she went after her and took the cage. When she raised it up and looked into it, a bird was inside. It had the plain ring in its bill. She took the ring and ran back with it, then waited for the little white dove to come and get the ring — but it didn't come.

She leant against a tree and as she stood there, it seemed as if the tree was getting soft and bending its branches

forwards. Then suddenly,
to her surprise, the
branches wrapped
around her and
became two
arms. She
stepped
forwards and
when she looked
round, the tree
had a face. It
then turned into
a handsome man,
who hugged and
kissed her and said,
"You have delivered
me from the power of

the old woman, who is a wicked witch. She had changed me into a tree except for two hours every day when I was a white dove. I could not speak of my enchantment and as long as she had the ring I couldn't get my human form back."

Then his servants and horses, who had also been changed into trees, were freed from the enchantment and stood beside him. The man led the girl to his kingdom, for he was a king's son, and they were married. The poor servant girl lived happily ever after as his princess.

Spindle, Shuttle and Needle

By the Brothers Grimm

Many people used to make thread from cotton using a spindle. They would weave the thread into cloth using a loom and a shuttle. A needle was then used to sew the cloth.

HERE WAS ONCE A GIRL whose father and mother died while she was still a little child. Her godmother lived all alone in a small house and earned money by spinning, weaving and sewing. The old woman took the child to live with her and taught her all she knew.

When the girl was fifteen years old, the old woman became ill. She called the child to her bedside, and said, "Dear girl, I feel my end drawing near. I leave you the little house, which will protect you from wind and weather, and my spindle, shuttle and needle, with which you can earn a living." Then she laid her hands on the girl's head, blessed her, and said, "Keep the love in your heart, and all will go well with you." Then she closed her eyes, and soon after she died.

The girl lived quite alone in the little house. She worked hard, spinning, weaving and sewing, and the blessing of the good old woman was on all that she did. It seemed as if the flax in the room increased of its own accord, and whenever she wove a piece of cloth or carpet, or made a shirt, she at once found a buyer who paid her lots of money for it, so that she could buy all she needed, and even had some to share with others.

About this time, the son of the king was travelling about the country looking for a bride. He was not allowed choose a poor one, but did not want to have a rich one. So he said, "I shall make a girl my wife if I can find one who is the poorest, and at the same time the richest."

When he came to the girl's village he

asked, as he did wherever he went, who was the richest and also the poorest girl in the place? The people in the village first named the richest. The poorest, they then said, was the girl who lived in the small house at the end of the village.

The rich girl was sitting in all her splendour before the door of her house, and when the prince approached her, she made him a low curtsey. He looked at her, said nothing, and rode on.

When the prince came to the house of the poor girl, she was not standing at the door, but sitting in her little room. He stopped his horse and saw through the window, through which the sun was shining, the girl sitting at her spinning

wheel, busily spinning.
The girl looked up, and
when she saw that the prince was
looking in, she blushed and went on
spinning. She carried on until the king's
son had ridden away, then she went to
the window and looked after him. When

she could see
him no longer she
sat back down to
work again.
  A saying that the old
woman had often
repeated came into her
mind, and she sang
these words to herself,
  "Spindle, my spindle,
haste, haste you away.
  And here to my house bring my
husband, I pray."
  And what do you think happened?
  The spindle sprang right out of her
hand in an instant, and out of the door,
and when, in her astonishment, she got

up and looked after it, she saw that it was dancing merrily into the open countryside, and drawing a shining golden thread after it.

Before long, the spindle had entirely vanished from the girl's sight. As she now had no spindle, the girl took the weaver's shuttle in her hand, sat down to her loom, and began to weave instead.

The spindle, however, danced always onwards, and just as the thread came to an end, it reached the prince.

"What do I see here?" he cried, "the spindle

379

wants to show me something!"

So the prince turned his horse around, and rode back, following the golden thread. Meanwhile, the girl was sitting at her work singing, "Shuttle, my shuttle, weave well this day, and guide my husband to me, I pray."

Immediately the shuttle sprang out of her hand and out by the door. Before the threshold, however, it began to weave a carpet that was more beautiful than anyone had ever seen. Lilies and roses blossomed on both sides of it, and on a golden ground in the centre, hares and rabbits, stags and deer bounded, while brightly coloured birds sat in the branches above. The shuttle leapt here and there, and everything seemed to grow on its own accord.

As the shuttle had run away, the girl sat down to sew. She held the needle in her hand and sang, "Needle, my needle, sharp, pointed and fine, prepare for a husband this house of mine."

Then the needle leapt out of her fingers, and flew everywhere about the room as quick as lightning. It was just as if invisible spirits were working. The needle covered tables and benches with green cloth in an instant, and the chairs with velvet, and hung the windows with beautiful silken curtains.

The needle had just put in the last stitch when the maiden saw through the window the white feathers of the prince's hat, whom the spindle had brought by the golden thread. He got off his horse, stepped over the carpet into the house. When he entered the room, there stood the maiden in her poor garments, but she shone out from them like a rose surrounded by leaves.

"You are the poorest and also the richest," he said to her. "Come with me, you shall be my bride."

She did not speak, but she gave him her hand. Then the prince gave her a kiss, lifted her on to his horse, and took her to the royal castle.

A great wedding took place soon after.
The spindle, shuttle and needle were kept
in the treasure chamber, and held in
great honour.

About the Artists

Smiljana Coh Books, stories and fairy tales are some of Smiljana's favourite things. She studied film animation in Zagreb, Croatia, and during her studies there began working as an illustrator. She is often asked to draw children, princesses and fairies — but for her sons she draws trains and buses.

The Flower Princess ★ The Unseen Bridegroom ★ The Twelve Dancing Princesses ★ Admetus and Alcestis The Twelve Brothers ★ The Dirty Shepherdess ★ The Old Woman in the Wood

Mélanie Florian French illustrator Mélanie has always had a passion for drawing and telling stories. Her favourite medium is watercolour, for the freshness, lightness and freedom it offers. Her work has been published worldwide, and she has also written and illustrated two books that have been published in several countries.

How Princess Angelica Took a Little Maid ★ The Princess and her Grandmother ★ Kate Crackernuts Tatterhood ★ Ozma and the Little Wizard ★ The Mother and Daughter who Worshipped the Sun

Marcin Piwowarski From a very young age Marcin began painting, and he now specializes in children's illustration. His style is energetic, with multicultural references. Marcin's work has now been published in the UK, Norway and the USA.

The Princess Emily ★ How the Princess was Beaten in a Race ★ The Three Dogs ★ The Sea-Hare Noel's Princess ★ The Ruby Prince ★ Maid Maleen ★ The Crow

Jennie Poh Jennie graduated from the Surrey Institute of Art and Design with a BA Honours in Fine Art, but illustration has always been her first love. She now illustrates children's books, greeting cards and gift wrap fulltime. Jennie finds inspiration from her childhood in Malaysia and also time spent living in the beautiful Norfolk countryside.

Work Hard and Do Well ★ The Fair Princess ★ The Princess and the Hare ★ Princess Peony The Twelve Huntsmen ★ The Princess and the Lion ★ Spindle, Shuttle and Needle

Kirsten Wilson As well as illustrating, Kirsten paints, prints, carves stone and makes jewellery. She graduated with a degree in Fine Jewellery Design and Manufacture from Central St Martins College of Art, London, and now makes bespoke pieces for customers all over the world.

The Minstrel's Song ★ Princess Hyacinth ★ The Princess and the Raven ★ The Swan Children of Lir Earl Mar's Daughter ★ Old Rinkrank ★ The Secret Princess ★ The Red Slippers

384